ZOE ANNE

FREEMAN

WHEN ROMANCE TURNS TO TERROR

FREEMAN

First published in Great Britain in 2019

Copyright ©2019

Zoe Anne has asserted her right under the Copyright Designs and Patents Act 1988 to be identified as the author of this work.

A CIP catalogue record for this book is available from the British Library.
This book is sold subject to the condition that it shall not by way of trade or otherwise be lent, resold, hired out or otherwise circulated without the publisher's prior consent in any form of binding or cover, other than that in which it is published and without a similar condition, including this condition being imposed on the subsequent purchaser.

Typeset in 11/16pt Sabon
Printed and bound in Great Britain

I am dedicating this book to my niece, Anna. Unknown to you, you gave me the light and love, and I love you zillions.

It's been emotional.

All characters are fictional, and no resemblance is intended to any living persons.

ABOUT THE AUTHOR

✦✦✦✦

Zoe Anne was on Boss Modelling books in 1993, years later in 1997 starred in Cosmopolitan Magazine winning the Face of the Future Competition in Manchester for London's Elite Modelling Agency. Zoe Anne also starred on ITV 2003 with Deane Gafney, Richard Blackwood and Samantha Fox. Zoe Anne was an IT girl for a while, in the celebrity status. Now she lives in solitary confinement in the Cotswolds and remains to do so. Zoe Anne has a passionate love for Animals. Zoe Anne has a Diploma working in the animal welfare industry looking after families pets in the area.

CHAPTER 1

✦✦✦✦

I'm the gregarious type; just out of college, still kissing random guys at nightclubs, bars, parties. I spend time with old friends from sixth form, but I'm losing contact one by one as time moves on.

I'm eager to learn media studies as well as business and finance, striving to become a success, commuting to London regularly to fail at interviews, with sweaty palms, shortness of breath when replying to questions I wasn't prepared for and where there were fifty other candidates mostly suited and booted in expensive attire.

Mother and father have put our house up for sale, wanting to upgrade to a bigger house in the same village in the countryside. My brother Austin, still in school, is six years younger than me and only interested in football. He is sugar-coated by our parents, who are not pushing him like they pushed me. Mother instilled in me the five Ps on repeat in my head: "preparation prevents piss poor performance".

At home searching the internet while the removal men hauled packed brown boxes up and downstairs to the removal truck, I sat in the corner of my pastel pink dimly-lit room at the top of the house, boxes everywhere, the bed resting against the wall waiting to be taken, my little work station on the old oak table, reading the internship position on the Mac: 'Whatever your major or programme, whether you are an undergrad or postgraduate, if you are interested in fields from advertising, finance, news, technology, clean energy, there is a place for you here'. Applying online, I got a response immediately.

Rummaging through boxes and packing a light suitcase, I headed straight to the railway station. Text to mother: *Gone to London xx.*

Seven years later: quintessentially, I'm sitting in the bar opposite the shiny blue tinted offices with my newspaper held up, hiding my face and natural curly blonde bobbed hair. I'm dressed in a navy knee-length dress, tan stockings, Louis Vuitton black high heels. I wipe a strand behind my lobe, big brown eyes blink, bite my full lips together. Nobody could see the stress I was feeling, energy zapped right out.

I did an internship for a year and made my way up through the business. Now I have a hectic managerial role, in sole charge of marketing editors, secretaries and sales assistants. Got a target deadline: 30 million prints to be ready in the morning. I have to think of something. Jerry is going to skin me alive if I don't get this in by 8pm tonight.

I peer over the newspaper, I look at the businessmen gathered round the bar laughing together, but I can't hear. This is my daily routine, part of the furniture now, escaping for lunch, ordering a latte, a bottle of sparkling water, a tuna salad with avocado and a mint dressing.

'Excuse me, could I have a word? My friend over there, see that one in the grey suit?'

'Uh, yes?'

'That one, there.'

'Yeah, I see him.'

'Ah, he really likes you. All he does is speak about you every day. He's driving us bonkers, so I thought I'd come over to see if you would put us out of our misery, and...'

'And what?'

'You would be doing us a kind favour if you would go out for dinner with him.'

'Absolutely not! I don't know him.'

'You do know he is one of London's leading barristers? Single, not bad looking, not as good looking as me, mind, but please say you will meet him for dinner?'

'He hasn't asked me. You're asking on his behalf.'

'The thing is, I think he believes you're out of his league.'

'If he thinks that then I probably am. If you don't mind, I would like to get back to my paper, in fact, I must go back to work.'

'Adam.'

'You're Adam?'

'No, him, he's Adam.'

'Ah, I see.'

'So, you'll have dinner with him?'

'I must go, excuse me.'

I grab my cream Christian Dior bag, stand and look up. Adam turns towards me, our eyes meet. I see a tanned neck and face. He smiles beguilingly, looks directly at me. I pick up my cream coat, leave the table and head for the side entrance so I don't have to walk past them. *Guess that told him!*

The August summer's humidity hits my body and curls stick to my face as I cross over Kensington High Street. I dash over the pedestrian crossing, walk through the colossal glass entrance past the concierge and hit the elevator button, not eager to face everyone on the fourth floor. Everybody stares through the office window, hearing Jerry's authoritarian voice. He shouts, galvanising us so that all 180 of us can hear:

'Ah, the wanderer returns.'

'Jerry, I'm on it.'

'Make sure you are.'

All of us are on a deadline tightrope. I look back at everyone with a horrid witch glow, squint my eyes.

Heads all back to their screens. My elbows rest on the mahogany table, my head in my hands as I stare blankly at the screen.

Jerry, you halfwit!

I tap YouTube, listening to Chopin softly play, gathering my thoughts on the finals for print.

Gravity doesn't seem to be pulling me out of this situation. The cover of one publication is wrong, upside down; But I've already pressed send and it's now 8pm There's no way out of this, my job will be kaput, I'm finished, everyone else left hours ago, including Jerry.

Nobody is at print until 2am. Feeling melancholy, I wrap my hair in a bun, grab my coat and bag, switch off the lights, set the alarm and lock the doors.

CHAPTER 2

✦✦✦✦

A hot summer's Friday evening: I head straight for the Bell. It's packed, the atmosphere buzzing, everyone out to enjoy themselves, happy faces laughing into other happy faces, whereas I'm suffering, disparity at its best, heart beating so hard like it is going to burst right out of me. I sigh, walk past through the crowds and head for the bar,

'Double vodka, straight up please.'

'Coming up.'

Look at the back of the pub where my table was, speakers are being put up, strobe lights flashing, a man is setting something up; Perhaps he's a live singer or it's open mic night. The drink doesn't touch the sides. I've never been in here in the evenings. *I hope it's not bloody karaoke!*

'Another one please.'

'Gotcha.'

'Thanks.'

'Might as well just ask for the bottle' I mutter, giggling to myself. Messing up my career, fuck it. I had had enough anyway and had an eerie feeling that something was not right. Lost in thought, convincing myself that I needed a new career anyway.

Wind of Change, The Scorpions, blasts my ear drums, and I'm blinking as the vodka hits the bloodline, dizzy, turning my aching neck around, scratching my back, tired of this dress. I just want to go home, take a hot shower and scream.

Then I feel the soft pull on my elbow and turn to face him, my eyes staring into his, his into mine. I bite my bottom lip.

'You're something else,' he says.

'Ha, you wouldn't be saying that if you knew what I'd done.'

'Have you been a naughty girl?'

'Yup.'

'Tell me?'

'Really, you don't want to know.'

'Oh, I think you should spill the beans, I definitely want to hear.'

'Seriously, you don't need to hear this.'

'Perhaps I can help. You do look on the pale side, are you okay?'

There must be some kind of way out of here by the

Watchtower blasts through the surround. My eyes are blinking; I'm trying to stay focused; I need to get out of here', the lyrics spinning through my head, I'm not wanting to have this conversation with him, I want to get out of here, go home, sleep, pick up my stuff from the office before anyone gets in tomorrow morning.

'I feel sick.'

'Come on, I've got you.'

'I'm fine.'

'You don't look fine.'

'Honestly, I'm fine.'

'Let me help you.'

'No thank you, I told you, I'm fine.'

'I'll walk you outside, you're all over the place.'

'Fine.'

'Wait here, I'll call a taxi for you, you're welcome by the way.'

'Why are you being so kind to me?'

'Because you are completely pissed.'

'Ha!'

'What's so funny?'

'You're being so authoritarian.'

I sit on the pavement on the side street by the pub, legs crossed at the side of the kerb. I lean over and rest my head on my bag and coat, hiccupping loudly, my mouth filling up with water. My head turns towards the grid and I vomit right into it.

My cream coat is being put over my shoulders. He's trying to spare any dignity I might have left.

'Sorry.'

'Ha! For what?'

'Being a complete mess and you being here watching.'

'I've seen worse.'

'You don't have to do this.'

'You don't usually come here at night.'

'I don't usually mess up my career.'

'What do you mean?'

'Completely fucked up.'

'Oh gosh, in what way?'

'The end of my career way.'

'Sophia, what have you done?'

'I, uh...'

'Tell me.'

'I'm a mess, it's over, that's all I can say.'

'Maybe I can help you.'

'Why would you?'

'Because even though you are a stubborn, stuck-up cow, you are still my boss.'

'Am I a cow?'

'Yes.'

'Oh, I'm sorry.'

'Sorry for throwing up on my shoes, or sorry for being a cow?'

'Sorry for both.'

'Wow, you're saying sorry!'

'Huh uh.'

'You got the keys?'

'Right here.'

'Let's go, come on.'

'Where?'

'To the office.'

'Why?'

'To sort out the mess you made.'

'It's too late.'

'Come on, it's never too late, get up.'

Reaching into my handbag for a tissue and wiping my mouth, I stand up and hold Jack's hand. I meet his gaze. Big blue eyes, straight blonde hair falling to his brow. Linking arms, we cross the street. Taxis honk their horns. Then Jack puts his arm round my shoulders.

CHAPTER 3

✦✦✦✦

'Perhaps she isn't right for me at all, she looks a total mess, acting like a teenager, knocking the drinks back and getting drunk'. I watch with interest, wanting to go over and introduce myself, but before I get a chance he walks over and beats me to it, lucky bastard. I turn to my drink on the bar for a moment, and when I look back I see the seats replaced by two women. I wonder where they were. The crowd's too busy to see and I am certainly not, scouring the place like a fool, but I want to tell her she is making a mistake.

I finish my drink and leave at the side entrance, and as I walk through the door there she is, sitting on the pavement throwing up. Oh my god, she is totally wasted. He's walking up to her, phone in hand, putting her coat around her shoulders, rescuing her – bastard! Watching them talking, looking into each other's eyes. Better let this one go. Watching them cross the street in disbelief, I think, she must be off her head with him, he must be eighteen, she needs a man, me'.

'What are you doing out here, did you see her, speak to her?'

'No, she's gone.'

'Well why didn't you say something before she left?' She was sitting at the bar alone and you didn't go over.'

'It's too late, she's gone off with that young bloke. He's way too young for her.'

'What are you going to do?'

'Nothing. Another one for the road?'

'Optimism my friend, you hear me?'

'Hmm, she just went to her offices with him at this time of night wasted, she was throwing up on the pavement.'

'Pretty sure it's fine mate, but he is kind of a catch.'

'Gary, I don't think he is gay, you will have to look somewhere else.'

'Leave my sexuality out of it. You have to admit he's fitter and younger than you.'

'You're not helping. I'm out of here.'

'Stay for another, it's on me, come on.'

'No, I'm calling it a night.'

'Adam, look, she's back.'

'Where?'

'At the bar.'

'Holy fuck.'

'So?'

'So?'

'So what?' Go over, stupid.'

'I'm thinking about it.'

'Just go over, ask if she's feeling better. Do I need to write all this down?'

'Fine.'

'This isn't happening; she looks damn beautiful'.

I muster the courage, heart racing, and walk towards her, nudging arms, trying to reach the other side of the bar. What am I going to say to her?

'Hey you, are you feeling better?'

'Ah, you're Adam, uh, hi, yes thanks. I take it you saw me earlier then?'

'Yes, you were with a young guy, is he here with you now?'

'He's working in my office.'

'Working?'

'Yes, it's a long story.'

'Well, I've got the time.'

'I'll give you the short version. I have a deadline to meet, things have gone wrong, I could be unemployed by tomorrow. The end. How are you?'

'Oh! Ok, I won't persist, but perhaps that's a good thing. I'm good thanks, can I get you a drink?'

'No thank you, what does that mean? Just asked the barman if he can get me some milk, I drank far too much earlier and I need a lot of caffeine.'

'May I take you out for dinner tomorrow and I'll try to explain what that means?'

'Oh Adam, I am really busy.'

'Busy doing what on a Saturday evening?

'Adam, I do not wish to be rude to you.'

'Then don't be.'

'I'm sorry.'

'So am I. I'll bid you goodnight then, as you are clearly not interested.'

'It's complicated, just...'

'You don't like me, I get it. Are you...?'

'Ha, I really hope you're not asking if I bat for the other side.'

'Well, it is confusing these days, you never know. Gary over there, the one who rudely asked you on my behalf without a warning to me I might add, he likes your colleague, he is... you know. Listen, you're beautiful and I would love to get to know you better.'

'Are you serious? You thought I was...'

'Just being a man. If you won't have dinner with me... look, please say you'll have dinner with me?'

'Okay.'

'Really?'

'Yes, I'm intrigued to know what that meant.'

'The Ivy at seven tomorrow, and I'll try and explain.'

'See you there Adam. Now I need to get back to the office.'

'See you tomorrow, goodnight Sophia.'

'Yes, you will, goodnight. And how do you know my name?'

CHAPTER 4

✦✦✦✦

'If I do this, you're going to tell Jerry I'm being promoted to leading editor, right?'

'Jack, you've only been with us a few weeks, I am afraid I can't do it.'

'You remembered my name then. Up to you – I do this, and you get me a promotion?'

'Can I offer you leading line manager?'

'Sophia come on, you know I got more skills than most of those editors put together.'

'I really can't, it's not the way Jerry works.'

'Your career is on the line and I can rectify it if you give me two hours.'

'I can rectify it, Jack.'

'If you do this then I'll ensure that everyone in the office stops calling you a witch.'

'Ha! And you think that you being leading editor before them will make you popular with them?'

'I don't think you have a choice.'

'I can just leave with my things and get a new job, somewhere else. What will you do Jack? You are just out of college.'

'I can get you out of this mess. I'm just out of university, not college thank you very much, and I'm older than I look.'

'How old are you?'

'It's irrelevant.'

'Come over here.'

'Are you flirting with me?'

'Maybe, come over here.'

'No.'

'Why not?'

'Because I am not taking advantage of someone who has been drinking and has vomit breath.'

'Oh my, you really are headstrong.'

'Does everyone do what you want them to do?'

'In work, yes.'

'It's ten thirty and we're not supposed to be at work.'

'You're in my office about to save my career, I'd call this territorial work.'

'But I am not your territory.'

'No, but you're working especially hard for me, and I'm a witch according to you!'

'Do you want me to do this? It's going to take two to three hours and time's pressing before they start at two.'

'Jack, I really cannot promote you to leading editor.'

'Fine, I am out of here.'

'Wait. You have my word that I'll hold a meeting with Jerry, with all three of us, and I'll see what I can do.'

'Or you can say you're resigning, and I'm the best candidate to take your role.'

'Then I may just take my things now, leave the role open and see who Jerry gives my position to.'

'You have a hold over Jerry and he listens to you, you know that.'

'How old are you, Jack?'

'Twenty-six.'

'You look younger.'

'You?'

'Me what?'

'How old are you?'

'Twenty-five, almost twenty-six.'

'See, you're younger than me with the leading manager role on all of us.'

'I worked here straight out of college and did a year's internship and worked my way up. It took me three years to be where I am because I fought and work from eight in the morning until eight at night, twelve hours a day seven days a week. I have no social life and no love life because I sleep and breathe for this company and quite frankly I have had enough of it, if I am being completely honest.'

'You are something else, like I said earlier, but if you want to jack it in, that's your choice.'

'Look, let's just work together on this. I'll call a meeting with Jerry first thing Monday morning and brief him first, how about that?'

'How about you brief him now? You're the one who sleeps and breathes for this place.'

'Fine, you work your magic on the editorial and I'll brief Jerry first thing. It's too late to do it now, you know it's late. A tad unprofessional isn't it?'

'Sophia.'

'Yes?'

'Brief him a draft now and we will both press send together once I've completed the changes.'

'Fine, I'll do a draft now. First I need coffee, you?'

'You're asking me if I want coffee?'

'Is that strange to you? How do you like it?'

'Pretty fucking awesome! Touch of milk and half a sugar please.'

'Coming up. Seeing as we're going to be here all night, I'll make a pot, see you in a jiffy. And Jack?'

'What?'

'Thank you ever so much.'

'Ha, you're not a complete witch after all, I knew you weren't.'

'You ain't seen nothing yet.'

'Where's that coffee?'

'Be right back.'

CHAPTER 5

✦✦✦✦

I'm feeling so happy that Jack saved my career and I'm going out on a date. My life is taking a nice turn for once, and I'm eager to see Adam and wonder why he thought I was batting for the other team. I'm sitting on the bed, lying back, thinking 'that's what people must think of me, no friends, no partner, no social life, working twenty-four seven, oh my God, I really need this date with him, I need a life and I am going to grab it with both hands, I deserve it, it's what everyone else is up to on a Saturday night'. Work has been my ethic; I have forgotten there's a life outside it.

I jump up, pour myself a glass of sauvignon, grab a pen and begin to write a bucket list. 1). Socialise and make friends 2). Date a lot 3). Book a holiday 4). Bungee jump 5). Skydive 6). Work less in the evenings). Stop being such a bitch to work colleagues 7). Go to the gym 8). Invite friends around for dinner (when I get some) 9). Eat more 10). Drink less 11). Be a tad late for my date 12).

In black stockings and matching black lingerie, I'm dancing around my bedroom to *The Power of Love* on full Surroundsound. Brushing my hair, body swaying to the rhythm. Searching through the three-door mirrored wardrobe, sliding the doors, throwing dresses onto the puff diamond grey bed. I pause, opt for a knee-length, sleeveless crushed black velvet knee length dress, ease into it, match it up with high heeled black and red Louis Vuittons from the dozens neatly paired on the top shelves. I look in the mirror, turn to see the rear view, like what I see. I grab a mirror and put the final touches to my make-up.

Having decided to walk to Marylebone Lane I look at my Smart watch: 6.50, plenty of time. Looking through the bay window and seeing a blue sky, I take a light pastel green coat from the rail in the double-doored hall cupboard and head down George Street in the direction of the Ivy. After a few minutes the humidity begins to make my hair curlier, tendrils are sticking to my cheeks and I'm perspiring with every step.

Taking off my coat, I glance up to see a dark blue cabriolet with the roof down, driven by a man with short ebony hair as he zooms past; I wish I was in that car right now. I look up at the now darkening sky, and small droplets of rain are falling lightly on my face. I look at my watch; eight minutes to my destination. Picking up my pace, the grey pavement getting wetter, I wave at a black cab: 'the Ivy please!'. He drives off, shouting, 'It's there love.'

Dashing up the road, I'm almost running. *Idiot, ugh.* The droplets are getting heavier and I'm now running in my high heels, holding my coat over my head and shoulders, eager to get to the main door. Making it, I stand under the archway to the big green double doors and try to push them open. I'm baffled – they're closed. Ugh! I turn and see a man sitting under cover at Café Blue, smiling in my direction.

'It's around the other side,' he says.

'Thank you'.

This is awkward. Heart pounding with adrenalin, soaking wet, hair stuck to my face, thunder roaring, I'm gasping for breath. I'm running around what seems like a castle to get to the main entrance around the corner.

Two men in black attire open the doors to me and I stare at the lady in reception, who is in black and white formal dress.

'Do you have a reservation?'

'Yes, do you have a bathroom?'

'What name is it?'

'I'm afraid I don't know the surname. Can I use your bathroom?'

'It's through the main restaurant.'

'Oh bugger.'

'The lady is with me.' Adam is looking in my direction, smiling. 'Can you get her a towel? She's a bit wet.'

'Very funny, Adam.'

'Why on earth did you not jump in a taxi?'

'It was a clear blue sky, I didn't expect the heavens to open and swallow me up.'

'Well, at least you made it.'

'I'm going to the ladies, be right back.'

'I'll be waiting at the table. Ask the maître d' to bring you to our table.'

'Thank you.'

'You're most welcome.'

Taking the towel out of the man's hand, he opens the door as I try to pat my hair dry, drying my arms and looking into my reflection: bright red face, mascara smudged under the lids, sighing aloud through my round lips, reaching down and drying my legs. Two women walk into the room:

'Oh poor you! It's just stopped, we waited in the car around the corner.'

'Yes, I went to the wrong entrance, why have closed doors there?'

'Yes, we saw you.'

'Hmm.'

'Lucy. And you are?'

'Uh, Sophia, nice to meet you.'

'You too.' The other lady is in the cubicle. Lucy is dressed immaculately in a long figure-hugging black dress, long straight blonde hair, big blue eyes holding out a tissue. I look at her and she wipes my eyes, her breath into mine, stepping back.

'Hmm thanks, but I got this, thank you.'

'You're welcome. Here, put some of this on, it will stop the redness.' Taking the powder out of her hand I smudge my cheeks with the brown compact make-up. Then I take out my rouge lipstick, scratch my back and look at the chandeliers through the mirror. Lucy is adding some of the powder. The toilet flushes.

'Thank you, Lucy I hope you both enjoy your evening.'

'Lovely to meet you, have fun.'

Adam is right outside, holding his elbow out. Taking his arm, he puts his other hand onto my hand. I whisper into his ear, 'I thought you said to meet you at the table?'

'You were quite a while in there, are you all right?'

'Yes, just got talking to a woman in there.'

'Really? You make friends quickly.'

'She just offered me some, ah it doesn't matter, but she leaned in and I thought she was going to kiss me for a second.'

'What? Who is she?'

'I don't know.'

The entire restaurant becomes eerily hushed, watching us walking arm in arm to our table. The maitre d' asks Adam, not looking in my direction, 'champagne list sir?'

'Dom Perignon Rosé 2002,' he says. I sit on the pastel orange leather corner seat, thighs sticking as I move around trying to get comfortable. I stare into his gaze, his dark eyes glistening, sitting facing me away from anyone else, attention totally on me. He stares at me, silently laughing.

'Sophia, will you stop fidgeting?'

'You try sitting here.'

'What's wrong?'

'My dress is wet through. My bottom is sticking to the leather.'

'I kind of like that.'

'What?'

'Excuse me, I'm sorry, I didn't mean to offend you.'

His eyes are twinkling, glistening into mine, smiling in a cavalier way. I peer down at the menu, wishing he wouldn't stare at me, thinking about my wet bottom. I let out a light breath through my nose, bite my lips and focus on the varieties on the menu, pensively nervous at his extraordinary comment. My first real dinner date and I'm wet through, embarrassed, hair stuck to my cheeks. I lightly comb my hair with my fingers, putting a curly wet strand behind my ear. This cannot be happening to me, it's bloody embarrassing. He will not be asking me out on a second date. Well, smartarse, I don't want I don't want another date anyway. Clever barrister, tanned olive skin, athletic physique, straight white teeth, soft kissable lips, small nose (bonus), wearing a navy-blue Savile Row suit and white shirt. I want him right now. Nope, very silly, keep your attention on your wet dress and the menu.

'What do you fancy?'

'Sea bass, you?'

'Nice choice, it will go well with the champagne.'

'So, you are a barrister.'

'That is correct.'

'What did you mean last night, that there's a possibility it may be a good thing?'

'What would you like to know?'

'How long have you worked as a barrister? And what you meant?'

'Hmm, cannot really discuss my work I'm afraid, it is complicated.'

'Pretty sure you know something I am unaware of.'

'I do, and you must know I put away criminals.'

'Oh, and there are criminals in my offices. Do you defend criminals as well as helping various clients?'

'In a nutshell yes. Do we have to have this conversation now? I really think we should change the subject.' I almost spit my champagne out but keeping my lips closed, I swallow the crisp, dry bubbles.

'I think it's inappropriate on our first dinner date, and the last thing I want to do is disappoint you.'

'Sure, we can change the subject. Where do you live?'

'Opposite Hyde Park, and your etchings?'

'George Street, that's why I walked, and the heavens opened.'

'Oh, not far at all. Have you been in here before?'

'No, and I went to the wrong entrance, just followed

my smart watch and it took me to the side doors. Very confusing especially in a thunderstorm which, by the looks of it, only caught me.'

'Ha, smart.'

'I think I'll be upgrading my smart watch.'

'Witty too.'

'Now you're being kind.'

'Kind is allegedly my middle name.'

'Not if you protect criminals.'

'Sophia, please don't.'

'Sorry, did I offend you?'

'Kind of.'

'My mouth has a mind of its own sometimes.'

'May we just stick to casual, and may I take you to mine afterwards?'

'Pardon?'

'I would like to show you something.'

'I'm intrigued.'

'Is that a yes?'

'It's a kind of yes, if this champagne gets me any drunker than I am now.'

'Hmm, facetious as well, I like it.'

'Do you?'

'I'll let you know.'

'Now who is being facetious?'

'You are smart, Sophia. What do you like to do in your spare time?'

'I, uh, I don't have any spare time.'

'You don't?'

'Just work I'm afraid.'

'I know the guy you work for.'

'You do, how?'

'I kind of work for a client of his. Like I said, it's complicated.'

'I thought we weren't discussing work?'

'You brought it up.'

'How is your sea bass?'

'Hmm, very nice thank you, how is your fillet?'

'Exquisite, thank you. More champagne?'

'Yes please, now I know you're trying to get me more drunk. Why aren't you having any more?'

'I'm driving.'

'I don't think I should drink any more after this, I'm not a drinker, goes straight to my head.'

'Yes I remember.'

'Oh please don't remind me, that was quite embarrassing.'

The food was delicious, the champagne too, the bubbles hitting my nose, my breath quickening. And Adam was the cherry on the cake.

CHAPTER 6

✦✦✦✦

'Sophia, you said eight thirty, where is he?'

'He will be here, it's only eight twenty-five.'

'You're always early, that's why you are where you are.'

'Jerry come on, he's on his way, he will be here.'

'Order coffee please.'

'I'll ring down, one sec.'

'Orange juice as well.'

'Okay, and orange juice too please.'

'Water too.'

'And water too, thank you, bye.'

'Jerry, they heard you anyway, gosh you're so bloody demanding!'

'Just letting them know who's the daddy.'

'Jerry, you are so funny!'

'Are you being funny?'

'Me? Never, not to you.'

'Good. I pay you a lot of fucking money, don't let this go to your head but you did a good job, well done. Open that envelope there, go on, open it.'

'Thank you, what is it?'

'Just bloody open it.'

Jack walks in smiling, showing his pearly whites, blonde straight hair, a side fringe which he flicks with his hand, big blue eyes. His hand reaches out to shake Jerry's, and Jerry stands to receive it.

'Nice of you to have this meeting, sir.'

'Sit down son, there take a seat next to Sophia.'

'Thank you sir.'

'Sir, ha! Call me Jerry mate.'

'Okay thanks Jerry.'

'Now late Friday night I got a brief about you, what do you want?'

'I thought it was in the briefing sir, I mean Jerry.'

'I know what was in the briefing son, but I want to know why you feel you should be promoted to leading editor.'

'Well I, uh, I have the right qualifications and I can do it.'

'Hang on a second, I read your profile son and you haven't been here long enough. What gives you the right to bloody want promoting at this tiny stage of your career? That's what I want to know. You opened that envelope yet?'

'Jerry, I don't understand?'

'Understand this. There is three hundred and fifty K and another hundred for your yearly bonus, now get your things and fuck off out of my building.'

Right there and then the drinks roll in on a silver trolley and I stare at Jack, not saying a word, walking to the elevator, holding clearly what is my last pay packet, wanting to cry, holding back the tears as the doors open on the fifth floor. Walking to my office, I clear it, put my files and diary in my black bag, pick up my purple lily plant off the windowsill and holding my mac in my arm, I close the brown door and walk towards the elevator, past everyone just getting ready for work at nine. The whole floor is silent, apart from a few whispers I can't hear.

What the fuck? Does he know about my fuck up, did someone tell him? Is he
angry I went to dinner with his friend, is he jealous, did he like or want me me? He's married. She used to call the office straight to my line at least once a week, strange that she hasn't called for months.

I walk home a few blocks dressed in a cream chemise and matching pencil skirt, not feeling good at all. Some of the staff are late for work, dashing up past me towards the offices, turning their heads, giving the plant I was carrying a double look.

I go into Café Blue, order a latte, and go through my

phone, re-reading the email I sent Jerry on Friday night. *Hi Jerry, it's me. I am letting you know that I completely fucked up today but don't worry, I have Jack in my office, a very competent young man indeed and I would like to promote him to an editor, he is capable of making clear decisions and is working till 1am correcting my errors! Sophia xx*

What an idiot!

Looking through the window, drinking my latte, I see Adam walk past with Lucy dressed in a sexy pastel blue knee-length figure-hugging dress, his arm linking hers. OMG what the fuck is happening to me? I am a complete wreck, a walking bloody disaster. I shake my head, I have got it wrong. I lean sideways to get a better look, nope, there they are, he is opening the passenger door of a silver Mercedes, then she smiles at him and he strokes her hair back round her ear. They drive off and I duck behind my plant, hoping he doesn't see me. Leaving it for a good ten minutes, I pay for my coffee and quickly head for home. Opening my blue front doors I slam them behind me, kick off my heels and waddle down the hallway on the thick cream carpet towards the modern chrome kitchen, opening the fridge, pouring myself a sauvignon for breakfast, drinking the glass down in one swig, then pour another, drink that in one and pour another. Walking round my lovely one-bedroom apartment, I don't care about Jerry and his tempestuous attitude, nor do I care about Adam and his pretty other woman. I scratch my unwashed bun out of my hair, shaking my hair so it falls over my face, gathering my thoughts, hoping life gets better with a glass in my hand. What the fuck are they doing in the morning? Does she live near me? Did he stay at hers last night? Did they have breakfast together?

Flopping down on my weathered grey sofa, still holding my half full glass of wine, I reminisce about Saturday night, being his girlfriend for a night. The sun's rays hit the mirror opposite, lights flash in my eyes, I put the glass on the oak coffee table and lie down, curling my legs up around in the fetal position. Vision of love, a one-night stand with the first man I gave myself to. The man that asked beguilingly if I would be his. Ha, what a joke! Almost twenty-six with no job, no boyfriend, been a bloody idiot on Friday at lunch, messing up the editorial and getting drunk. I pull the cream pillow over my face, crying and screaming into it so the neighbours can't hear, or think I'm being murdered, calling the police with a false alarm. That's all I need, another episode of Monday mania!

Phone beeps in my bag in the hall. I get up, walking unsteadily towards it.

Text from Adam: *I miss you.*

Text to Adam: *I don't miss you.*

Adam: *Really?*

Me: *Yes.*

Adam: *Fine.*

Me: *Fine.*

Another text from a number I don't recognise: *There was a man with a colossal bunch of flowers in your office. Jack xx*

Text from Jack: *I don't have your job! I got promoted to leading editor, start next week, I am so sorry, plus your office is empty. Jack xx.*

Me: *Jerry will fill it asap, by the way, who are the flowers from, is there a note? X.*

Jack: *No clue I'm afraid, no note, he left them on your desk and I don't see him any more. Jack xx.*

Good. Jerry will see the massive bunch of flowers, a pre-birthday present. Jerry always sends me flowers on my birthday, bet he ordered them and forgot. Bastard. Bet he fills my office up right away, ugh! OMG it's my bloody birthday on Saturday, better call mother and pack a suitcase for the weekend, yup I'll drive up on Saturday morning say I have a long weekend off work, stay until Tuesday, yup. Oh fuck, what if mother sent them? And why do I get bunches of bloody flowers every year? My name isn't bloody hyacinth!

Better call mother.

'Hello?'

'Hi Mum, I'm coming up Saturday morning for a long weekend.'

'Are you drunk?'

'No, why?'

'Are you crying?'

'No, I'm calling you from work, I have a dreadful cold, eyes running, nose etc.'

'You sound awful love, how are they treating you there, are you sure you're okay?'

'Yes, see you on Saturday and thank you for the flowers, bye.'

I close my wet eyes, thinking about Adam. Why is he with another woman, why was he touching her? Was she his real partner? Did he take her back to his, slowly making love to her? Floods of memories spin around my head: The concierge opening the doors for us leaving the Ivy, Adam opening the Porsche cabriolet door for me, pressing a silver button for the roof to unfold, driving past my house, me saying, 'That's me, right there, that one.' Driving down Edgware road, turning onto Cabbell Street, the end red townhouse opposite Hyde Park. Walking through the shining white marble entrance, up a white marble spiral staircase. Adam sliding off my coat, taking my hand, opening the huge triple glass doors and leading me into the spacious lounge. 'Come over here, sit on the terrace, you can hear the concert and see it, drink?' 'Oh yes please, wow this is amazing.' UB40 singing Red Red Wine, the sound so loud like we had front row tickets, but we're sitting on the highest floor of this beautiful old building. Dire Straits start with their guitars, Money for Nothing. Adam and I having our own party, Adam filling the champagne flutes, taking my hand, twirling me around, bringing my body closer into his, dancing with me, nodding, miming into a flute to the lyrics. My arms waving in the air on the pretty terrace with six-foot-tall, rounded moss. Six of them, the smell so fresh. Dizzy, I sit down laughing at Adam unbuttoning his shirt a couple at a time whilst he dances and waves his free hand in the air.

'This is amazing Adam, I love it.'

'This is what I wanted to show you.'

'Thank you.'

'No, thank you for letting me finally take you for dinner. I have a confession to make. You see, every lunch time, I watched you sit in the corner ordering the same food, reading the same paper every day for months. I made my secretary make sure twelve thirty to one thirty my diary was kept free. I had to see you, even if you did always hide your face in the paper. Why do you do that?'

'You mean you have been noticing for me for... how long did you say?'

'I said a while.' I stand up to meet his gaze. 'How long, Adam?'

'A couple of months.'

'I had absolutely no idea.'

'Well you wouldn't with the paper stuck to your face. How do you read like that?'

'It's a way to keep my colleagues away from me whilst I have lunch, to hide, to escape work and my deadlines, I work twenty-four seven for that company.'

'May I kiss you?' Adam interrupted, his soft fingers

over my mouth, hushing me from talking about boring work stuff.

'Huh, uh yes.'

Toyah's *It's a Mystery* blasts through Hyde Park and I feel his power as he holds my hand and dances with me to the rock star in the distance. Goosebumps, waves of coolness and electricity go right through my entire body from my feet up to my head as his lips softly hold onto mine. Then he stops, holding my chin, watching my eyes, and then kisses me again exactly like the first time, pulling me into the warmth of his electric heat as the breeze cools me, hair blowing in the gentle wind. We dance slowly to someone covering Prince's *Purple Rain*; movements, aesthetic and symbolic value, sharing each other's motions, dancing slowly, pushing my body backwards. He holds me with one arm, flexing my supple body. Trusting him, I turn to face him, lifting my head up, bringing me home into him again.

'I want you, but I want you the right way. Come with me, Sophia.'

'Adam, I uh, I am a...'

'You're a virgin?'

'Yes, you're going to be the first if we do this.'

'How old are you?'

'Does that matter?'

'If we're going to do this, then yes.'

'How old do you think I am?'

'Twenty-four, five?'

'Yes, twenty-five, good guess.'

'Come inside. Here, take my hand, let's just sit on the sofa and talk.'

'Talk about what? Am I too old, too young, tell me?'

'It's nothing to do with that.'

Sitting down on the huge, ruby red, soft, sofa, he grabs another bottle and passes me a tumbler of sparkling water.

'Drink it up, you need more water, I want you sober. You drank way too much.'

'Adam I am fine, honestly.'

'There is no rush, Sophia.'

'Are you mad at me for something?'

'It's not you.'

'Oh my gosh, it's not you, it's me, right? Are we doing this?'

'Doing what? No, I haven't been with anyone like you before, that's all.'

'What's wrong with me?'

'Nothing, nothing at all.'

'Then kiss me or tell me if I am doing something wrong.'

'Sophia look, just wait, there is no hurry. Why are you in such a rush for me to take you?'

'I'm in no rush, believe me, but I want you, you're not the first man I have kissed.'

'Stop it.'

'Stop what?'

'Trying to make yourself experienced, there really is no need.'

'Why are you laughing Adam?'

'Because you look kind of cute when you're angry.'

'I'm not angry, I just uh, I just want you, I never wanted anyone ever before. I wasn't ready years ago and I've been working three straight years with no life whatsoever, twelve-hour days seven days a week for a very egotistical misogynistic twerp.'

'Are you finished?'

'Huh yeah, that felt good. Where are you going?'

'To put some music on.'

'Okay, what are you putting on?'

Standing up necking the water in one, pouring myself another, I walk over to
him, putting my glass on the side table and my arms around his shoulders. I look at my glass next to the silver stacks of music turntables separated in their own mahogany casings.

'You like the Eagles?'

'I'm too young for them.'

'Ha, you're very funny.'

'Hotel California is my favourite.'

'Mine too, that's it, let's listen. Dance with me?' He pulls me close, wrapping his arms around my waist, then pushes me backwards, slowly picking me up with his hands, my head bowed down to meet his, smiling into his eyes, twirling me round in the air. I wrap my legs around his waist, bodies locking onto each other. Slowly we dance round the floor to the piano, my legs slide down and we both dance with air guitars and tune with no lyrics. Heads banging, nodding up and down to the music. I burst out laughing at his movements and he falls over laughing. My phone beeps, taking me out of this trance.

Text from Adam: *Where are you?*

Text to Adam: *Why?*

Adam: *Why aren't you at work?*

Me: *That's really none of your business.*

CHAPTER 7

✦✦✦✦

Text from Jerry: *Sophia, have the whole week off. Your job is safe, can't replace you and don't want to. Happy birthday and don't fuck up again. Jerry.*

Text to Jerry: *I am very sorry. Thank you, Jerry.*

Jerry: *You're worth your weight in gold.*

Me: *Thank you.*

I rub my eyes and look in the mirror. Coffee – I need lots of caffeine. Why the heck is he such a stubborn, horrid man? Why did he embarrass me in front of Jack, why is he offering me my job back? It's totally not like him to re-hire anyone, I have seen him in action, why is he doing this?

Standing in the kitchen, I switch on the Delonghi Magnifica coffee machine. The beans crush inside. I put the glass espresso underneath, tapping the marble worktop, biting my bottom lip, not being able to get him out of my head. Nothing's working, the wine didn't work, just got a splitting headache. I reach for the drawer that has all my medicine in and take out some paracetamol, opening the chrome fridge and drinking sparkling water right out of the bottle. The doorbell rings. Dashing through the hall, opening the side of the double doors, a huge bunch of white roses in my face:

'Sophia Evans?'

'Yes, that's me.'

'Delivery for you.'

'Who from?'

'I don't know, just the delivery driver.'

'For whom?'

'Are you going to take them? They're heavy, here.'

'Thank you.'

'The card's in the vase.'

'I got it, thank you.'

Standing in the hall, I put the flowers down, eager to find the card, and my skirt splits behind. Ignoring the tear, I count the pretty white roses one at a time with my forefinger, losing count, starting over again. Too many to count. Must be Jerry's apology, laughing at him and me. I shake my head in disbelief. You're giving me my birthday present, Jerry, I know you too well. Reaching for the white envelope, I smile and tear it open, waiting to read his apology for being such a horrid boss, or just a happy birthday.

Dear Sophia, happy pre-birthday, really miss you, Adam xxx. How on earth does he know my birthday? I pick up the vase, open the double doors and put them straight into the black trash bin on the bijou patio. Phone beeps in the lounge and I shut the doors, head back in and pick up the phone.

Text from Adam: *Why did you put the flowers in the bin? Adam*

Me: *Are you spying on me?*

Adam: *Can I come in?*

Me: *Why do you want to come in?*

Adam: *To see you, why do you think?*

Me: *Absolutely no way.*

Adam: *Why are you being like this?*

Me: *I saw you with her.*

Adam: *It's not what you think, let me come in please?*

Me: *I saw you with her!*

Adam: *Sophia please let me come in, I am standing at your front door.*

Me: *I am not dressed, give me two minutes.*

Adam: *I have seen you naked, open the door please?*

Me: *Wait!*

Dashing through the hall into the bedroom, I throw off my torn skirt and replace it with a pair of black trousers, almost falling over and getting my leg stuck. Why the bugger is he here? I dash back down the hall and my phone beeps from the bedroom. I run back to reach for it, run back down the hall and open the door.

'Hi, why is your face so red? Are you going to accept the flowers?'

'I don't know yet, because I've been running around getting changed.'

'Why have you changed?'

'A long story.'

'Was someone here?'

'Absolutely not.' Adam is dressed so handsomely, so casually with a blue sweater draped around his shoulders loosely tied in front.

'Have you been crying?'

'What's with all the questions Adam? I thought you wanted to explain your girlfriend situation to me. You can, I'll listen and then I would like you to leave please.'

'Sophia, she is not my girlfriend, she is a client and I cannot discuss client confidentiality with you.'

'Ha! Pull the other one'

'If she was my girlfriend, why am I here with the flowers in my hand, waiting for you to take them?'

'I'm not sure I want to take them.'

'Why am I here, if she was with me?'

'You stroked her face.'

'She was upset.'

'She didn't look upset.'

'Are you going to let me in?'

'You have five minutes.'

I walk into the lounge and sit down, curling my legs up in the black trousers. He puts the flowers down on the side cabinet and sits opposite me with the coffee table separating us.

'You look so beautiful.'

'Who is she to you? She was the woman in the ladies on Saturday, Lucy right?'

'Ah yes, she is a client. Look I had to pick her up. All I can tell you is that she is in a very awkward situation.'

'It didn't look that awkward, in fact it looked quite sticky.'

'What does that mean?'

'You know what that means.'

'Why don't you believe a word I am saying?'

'Because.'

'Because?'

'Looked very combustible to me.'

'I wouldn't be here if I was with another woman. Why aren't you at work?'

'I have the week off. How do you know it's my birthday?'

'You told me on Saturday, do you remember everything?'

'Of course I do.'

'Tell me?'

'Adam believe me, I remember everything, almost.'

'Almost? Tell me.'

'Yes. Driving from the Ivy is a bit of a blur, I remember walking up the endless stairs on your ridiculous staircase and everything from then. Why you don't have a lift?'

'The exercise, plus it's a listed building. Have you been drinking?'

'I had a glass with lunch.'

'What did you eat?'

'Wine.'

'You ate wine? Ha, you're funny, let me take you for a real lunch.'

'Now?'

'Yes, now!'

'Nobu?'

'Yes, I'll just change out of these and slip something else on.'

'You're fine like that.'

'Adam it's red hot outside, I'll be two ticks.'

'Okay I'll make a reservation.'

'Okay.'

CHAPTER 8

✦✦✦✦

I opt for a cream linen knee-length skirt. Hearing footsteps in the corridor, I don't want to turn around. I know he is watching me. As he walks past, I turn around.

'You have any water?'

'Help yourself.'

'How are you alive?'

'What?'

'Living off water, wine and what's this, ooh vodka.'

'I haven't been shopping. There's fresh coffee, just press the green button, it's automatic.'

'Yeah, I have the same, water will do. You ready?'

'Yup, ready.'

'Let's go.'

I take his hand along the pastel green newly painted corridor, grab my black bag from underneath the coat rail and shut the doors behind. He opens the silver Mercedes passenger door and I sit with both legs together, feet identical, as demurely as possible. He smiles at me as he closes the door and I look up to meet him, smiling back and biting my bottom lip.

Jerry is sitting in a corner suite on our left with three other businessmen. He peers over at me, eyes squinting at me, then his head turns back to focus on his meeting. The atmosphere is buzzing with people, raising their wine glasses, chatting busily, laughing at each other, Japanese chefs cooking teppanyaki in front of a square table, waiters pouring pots of chai.

'That's who you work for, he's a total galvanising bigot.'

'I know.'

'I don't want you working for him.'

'I beg your pardon?'

'I just don't like him.'

'I've worked for him for seven years, pays the bills.'

'I know what position you're in, you can work anywhere.'

'Quite content, thank you.'

'I'm just saying that that's what I meant on Friday.'

'Am I supposed to find another job because you don't like him? What is he up to, tell me?'

'You don't know him like I do.'

'I know him very well thank you.'

'Sophia, not outside of work you don't.'

'Do you know something that I don't?'

'Promise you will look for somewhere else. I'm pretty sure you'd be much better off if you didn't work for him, that's all.'

'I don't know him outside of work as you already know. I know he is married, but I've never seen her. Naturally I know her voice when she calls and screams at me to get him on the phone right away. God knows why she gets through to my line.'

'That's her, this morning, I shouldn't say anything more.'

'That's his wife?'

'Keep your voice down, please.'

'She is far too pretty to be with him, have you seen his stomach?'

'Sophia, that's enough, I really shouldn't have said anything.'

'How does he know you, are you in trouble?'

'What? No.'

'So, she is your client. I want to know what's going on.'

'Okay but not here, let's eat.'

'Okay, I'll choose the sushi, phew.'

'I'll have the seafood. He's coming over, Sophia let me do the talking.'

'Hello, you two, what a pleasant surprise.'

I nod and smile, and Adam stands up formally shaking his hand. The two stares blankly into each-other's eyes.

Perplexed at their hostility, I sit there looking up at them whispering into one another's ears. What are these two talking about? Why is she his client and yet they're like best friends, isn't that illegal?

Jerry: five foot six, chubby physique, huge stomach almost popping the buttons on his white shirt, short jet-black hair, pale skin, deep-set brown eyes, small facial features, kind of handsome until he opens his mouth, with veneers too big for it. Jerry nods at me, shakes Adam's hand, walks off towards reception. I'm pondering whilst Adam texts on his phone. Why has Jerry re-hired me? Something's up, I can feel my empty stomach twist in my gut. Why does Adam want me out of the way, why is Jerry's wife my boyfriend's client? Are these two just discussing something?

'More wine?'

'Yes please.'

'Are you okay, what are you thinking about?'

'Eh, mother, I said I'd visit on Saturday for a long weekend. My birthday, it's a family ritual.'

'Really, can family rituals be broken?'

CHAPTER 9

✦✦✦✦

Elizabeth Evans, dressed in white linen trousers and a pink poncho, short blonde hair, brown eyes, olive skin, is waiting at the beige door of the Apple Tree coffee shop in the village and pointing at an outside table. Her friend Mary, in denims and a black sweater, has a grey Gucci scarf draped around her clavicle. Her silver, almost grey hair curls neatly at her jaw.

'Tea, coffee?'

'Black coffee please Lizzie, so kind of you. I'll wait here outside to save the table, that one there okay?'

'Yes I'll go and order, would you like a cake?'

'No thank you.'

'That was very fast, excellent service.'

'They'll be out in a jiffy. I ordered a cream ice bun too.'

'Splendid darling. You know Andrew cost me a fortune putting him through Cambridge. He's been unemployed for years and of course I pay for his flat in Clapham Junction, to keep him going whilst searching for jobs. Finally, he had an interview with Saint James.'

'Oh, that's good, the Cirencester branch?'

'No, the London branch. Of course, I do worry if he's going to make it. The thing is, James' place takes a huge cut and Andrew jumps around so savvy after Cambridge, one bar job to another that doesn't pay a lot. Then there's Rebecca asking for twenty K. Of course, I gave it to her; she said Rachel doesn't need it, she's invested in bitcoins you know, I don't trust the web at all, do you?'

'Bitcoins?'

'Yes, the web currency, I think that that's what Rebecca said, I must have a look into it. She also said Rachel has invested two hundred and fifty thousand in the web money, most confusing isn't it?'

'Baffling! Sophia is very successful you know; she has a managerial role for Mitro Advertising in London, earns a fortune. Unlike her brother Austin, he's in rehab in Australia, an hour's drive from the coast, costing us a bloody fortune, it's the most expensive rehabilitation suite there. He's been there six months. He has wi-fi there so we can keep tabs on him. I do worry he'll come out next week and fall right back into the wrong crowd. I wish he would just come home. We're flying out next week, must try to persuade him to come home, it's winter there.'

'That's terrible! You must bring him home with you and put him into the Priory, it's very good there. Did you know my eldest is quite a success story? Doesn't have a regular lady friend yet, most extravagant.'

'Oh, jolly good. The sun's trying to break through. What a splendid day yesterday, I put my washing on the line this morning, that's why I was late getting to you. It's been years since we did this, must do it more often.'

'Yes we must. My decking is slippery, needs jet-washing. The barbecue doesn't work, I'll have to get a new one for Saturday. Would your family join us for Rebecca's 21st party this Saturday?'

'Hello ladies, which one is having the black coffee?'

'Here darling.'

'There you are.'

'Thank you, oh, that ice bun does look yummy.'

'Would you like half?'

'No thank you, I'm trying to eat less sugar. You know keeping fit at my age is most important. My doctor tells me my cholesterol is far too high, blood-pressure too.'

'Oh, I always eat cake with tea in the mornings, it's my guilty pleasure you know.'

'Where is Austin actually?'

'New South Wales, he went back packing a year ago. I do worry about him. He sent us an email telling us he needed ten thousand dollars to pay a dealer.'

'Elizabeth, what for?'

'Ice, they call it. We investigated it, it's Australia's

equivalent of cocaine we think, very addictive. He said they put a gun to his head and he had 24 hours to pay or he would be bloody shot. We were devastated.'

'Oh, terrifying, absolutely dreadful, poor Austin! How old is he again?'

'Nineteen. Not the best judge of characters, so it seems!'

'Far too young, but at that age you know, they get up to bloody all sorts. Did you know Rebecca had to be put in the Priory last year. A loose cannon she was, addicted to alcohol and cocaine, put me through bloody hell and back. I do hope she isn't doing anything ridiculous with the twenty K, she said she needed it for a deposit on a farmhouse she'd got her eye on, it's not too far you know.'

'Sounds very nice. Must persuade Austin to come home with us, that's what Frank and I'll do.'

'Oh, you must.'

'Hey ladies, can I get you anything else?'

'Another coffee? No, please can I have some hot water and a slice of lemon?'

'I'll have another tea please.'

CHAPTER 10

✦✦✦✦

'I must get back to work, let me take you home. Ready?'

'Ready.'

'Excellent, let's go. Where's my sweater? Ah, must be in the car.'

'Adam, how do you know Jerry, and why are you talking to him when you said that his wife is your client?'

'You're not going to let this lie, are you?'

'No.'

'It's complicated Sophia, that's all I can tell you.'

'In what way?'

'In the way that I cannot discuss the situation with you.'

'But...'

'Please leave it, it's work. The less you know the better all around.'

'Why did you impose the idea of me not working for him then, can you answer that honestly?'

'As I said, I don't like him, he's trouble and not a nice person. That's why I would like you to leave, find something else, somewhere else, anywhere but there.'

'I just work there, keep myself to myself and like I said, it pays the bills.'

'Come on, you can work anywhere, talent like you, you deserve the best.'

'I am content, but if it will make you feel better, I'll look for another window of opportunity somewhere else.'

'Thank you. I like the way you're warming to the idea.'

'Well if he's as bad as you're making him out to be, I don't wish to work for such a bad person. I know he's horrid at work, pushes me to do all the leg work, I practically do everything. Pretty sure now I am way too overworked and underpaid.'

'How much do you earn?'

'Adam, please!'

'Go on.'

'No, thank you for lunch.'

'Wait.'

'What?'

'Kiss me.'

I lean over and kiss him softly, turning around to open my door. Adam rushes round, pulling me into the air, pulling my body into his, wrapping his arms around my shoulders, smiling at me.

'I'll call you later.'

'Okay.'

'Bye.'

'Bye.'

As I enter the freshly-painted doors, my phone beeps. Putting my handbag on the floor, I reach for the phone, hitting my bottom on the side of the doors and pushing them behind me. Oh shit, bloody hell, my skirt! There's a blue streak down the side of my bottom and thigh. Bugger!

Dashing down the hall with my phone in my hand and leaving it on the marble worktop, I take off my skirt and look into the cupboard for liquid to spread over it, then put it into the sink, fill it up with hot water and scrub the linen. Peering over my left shoulder, I see the painter walking up the back-garden pathway. I run into the bedroom, pulling the cream blinds down, and reach into the mirrored wardrobe, opening the left one. I opt for some navy-blue linen trousers and a white T-shirt. Then I hear the water splashing on the grey marble kitchen floor. Holy shit! Phone beeps twice. I stop the tap, grabbing a towel from the drawer and mopping up the water.

Text from Adam: *You look incredible, missing you already. Adam x*

Text from Adam: *Oh dear, better buy you a new skirt! Adam x*

I watch the painter do the external on the back. Over the next couple of days, I do a few trips to the supermarket, fill up the freezer and pack the fridge with eggs, salad and enough for the next week. Then I go to the phone shop to see the latest deals.

My phone beeps in my hand.

Text from Adam: *Got to go to Spain re work, I'll be away a couple of days. Adam X*

At home, shaking my head and sighing at the phone, I slide it onto the worktop and stack the cupboards with more shopping. Days past, more shopping, bought the latest iPhone 10 in the store. Then at home I pack a light gold suitcase for the weekend and phone Julie, wanting to tell her about everything.

'Hey this is Jules, leave a message after my beep… beeeeeep! Ha, you know what to do.'

'Hey it's me. I thought you said you wanted to visit sometime, call me back, miss you so much, mwah!'

Text from Jack: *Bell 6pm, fancy a drink? Jack. X.*

Me: *Hmm, not sure. Sophia xx.*

Jack: *Come on, it's dress down Friday, Jerry announced you have the week off, but you're not drinking vodka, like you knocked back last Friday. Jack X.*

Me: *You're on. Sophia xx.*

I'm eager to hear the latest gossip. I want to see Jack to hear the news and try to stick to some on my bucket list. I look down it: 1). Socialise and make new friends. Look at my watch: 15:30, plenty of time. I walk to the bathroom, run a tap on the freestanding Jacuzzi, sipping water out of the bottle and adding some coconut oil to the water. I reminisce about my first night with him, the way he watched me, biting my lip.

I stare into the mirror at my reflection opposite the tub, slide off my denims and pull my pink Versace top off over my head, neatly putting them on the pouffe on the thick cream carpet. I step into the hot water, laying my head back and smiling as I think about last Saturday night.

Sitting on the ruby red sofa suite, he takes my hand, pulling me close, leading me down a wooden staircase, opening a huge stained wooden door. 'Stand there, against the wall.' I gasp for air, looking at the huge white walls, searching the room. There's nothing but a huge white bed, long thick white fabric curtains, automatically drawing. Adam is at the side of the door, pressing a silver and black panel. Chopin starts playing quietly through speakers I cannot see, Surround sound. Adam walks back to me, unbuttoning his navy trousers, looking at me. My legs start shaking as he takes his pants down his muscular legs. I look away, biting my lips together at the side. He holds my hand, leading me to the white bed; it seems to take ages to get to it. He walks me slowly over the soft white fluffy carpet, sliding off my black dress, unbuttoning my black bra, pulling my black Victoria's Secret briefs off and pressing me against the cold wall.

'Stand there, I want to see you.'

'Huh, what?'

'Come, sit down with me.'

'Ah, okay.'

'Lie with me.'

Gently stroking my inner legs with the oil creates sheens of bubbles over my olive tanned legs; the crystal light above catches glimpses of sliding bubbles. I sigh as my breath quickens with the memory of Adam laying me down softly on his white linen Queen sized bed, smelling the aroma of the fresh creaseless linen. He pulls me up to his face with his strong dark tanned arms, staring into my eyes, kissing me, looking into my soul, kissing me again, kissing my neck, making me gasp and sigh 'ah, ah', coming back up still kissing me all over my ear and jawline, then looking into me seeing my love reaction. My eyes are wide open, blinking as my breathing feels like it's out of control. He reaches into me again, kissing my lips ever so softly, taking my bottom lip, nibbling on it, shutting my eyes...

'Ready?'

'Ah, yes.'

'Open your eyes.'

'Okay.'

'I am going to take you and you'll be mine forever,' he whispers into my ear.

'Ah, okay.'

'Not yet.'

'What?' I sit up slowly and watch him move away.

His head is going down to kiss my small breasts, cupping them into his hands, softly licking around my areolae.

'Lie back down.' He pushes my shoulders back softly down on his bed.

'Ah!' I sigh as Adam bites my stockings, pulling them down with his full lips, making me quiver, shivering with anticipation, kissing my toes, all the way up my inner legs, holding them apart, coming back up, kissing my hip bone, his tongue licking around my belly button. He kisses me in the centre of my torso, up to my clavicle, tongue stroking to the left part, then to the right, licking under my jaw, kissing my lips again, harder this time. Our breath quickens together, his hands cupping the back of my neck, gently pulling my hair in his hands.

'Ready?'

'Yes.'

'Louder.'

'Ah, ah, ah, yes!' He slowly teases my wet labia and his thick girth presses into me, entering me, sliding in with one soft push, holding my neck up to his hot breath as I scream out loud right into his mouth, staring into his eyes. My breath almost stops as he pulls out, then back inside of me, 'Ah, ah, ah, ah, ah, ah, ah, ah Adam!'

Eyes locked onto one another, sweat dropping from his brow, my body shaking uncontrollably, goosebumps all over our hot sweaty bodies. He stays inside me, holding me tightly, our breath still entwined and slowing down as we gaze into each other.

'You okay?'

'Yes.'

He kisses me softly, eyes blinking out of control. There are flashes of darkness and light and my breath quickens again, mouth open, breathing uncontrollably, biting my bottom lip. I feel dizzy like I am about to faint. I'm trying to keep my head and neck from moving around but I can't. He pulls out of me slowly, staring at me, watching my body shake, my hands at the side holding onto the crisp linen.

'I really need some water.'

'Be right back.' I sit up, holding my knees in my arms, looking at the huge wet patch in the middle of the bed, legs still shaking, toes pressed together, looking at the droplets of blood.

'Your water.'

'I am sorry.'

'Sorry for what?'

'Look at your bed.'

'Was to be expected, don't apologise.'

Leaning onto the bed, he takes the empty glass out of my hand, then lies down and holds me tightly, so tender. Bodies locked together, covering us, wrapping us with the top of the duvet.

CHAPTER 11

✦✦✦✦

Text from Jack: *Where are you? Jack.*

Me: *On my way, Sophia xx.*

Jack: *Okay.*

I'm dressed casually in my navy linen trousers and a white T-shirt unwashed from a few days ago, hair in a bun, blue and white flats, walking up to the pub. Wondering how Jack's getting on. Is he excited about his new position on Monday?

Entering the pub, half as full as last Friday, I see Jack waving from where I had lunch every day. He's with three other people who have their backs to me; I signal back, miming I am getting a drink at the bar. Jack stands and walks towards me.

'Well?'

'Well what?'

'Jerry said you're back but having the week off, said you deserved a holiday.'

'I'm having a week off? Is that what he said to everybody?'

'Yes. What was that about Monday morning?'

'Jack, one thing you need to know is that he is a flippant bugger.'

'Got it. Come over here with us.'

'Who are you with?'

'Some of your fans.'

'Oh, you don't mean the fans that hate me, do you?'

'They certainly don't hate you, they bloody love you. Come on, they're all lovely, you'll see. Stop being such a stuck-up cow.'

'I most certainly am not! Look at what I am wearing!'

'Never seen you look so casual, there's something different about you. What have you done, changed your hair or something?'

'Nothing, just plain old me, I'm afraid.' I'm holding a glass of Chilean Sauvignon in my right hand, nodding my head and smiling, gesturing with my left – let's go.

'Hi guys.'

'Hey there stranger.'

'Hey, how are you?'

'Heard you lost your job, then you were on holiday, been anywhere nice?' Rebecca asks sarcastically, but she's smiling as she indicates to sit next to her.

'Okay, one at a time. No, I'm having the week off,

didn't want to let my lily plant die in my office whilst I wasn't there. You're all stuck with me for the foreseeable future, I'm afraid.'

'Sophia, we adore you, we all know you haven't got time for any of us over there. You do everything, no wonder you're having a week off. When was the last time you had a holiday?'

'Mm… I can't remember if I'm totally honest.'

'Well we, I, have worked for you, I mean for Jerry as well you, for four years and we get holidays, don't we?'

All three nod with approval, shaking their heads with pure happiness. Allan, a thirty-year-old editor, Clare and Rebecca nodding too.

'Yes, I know you from way back in the day, knew it was you.'

'You do?'

'Yes, I know where you're from, you were just leaving school, when I started. Our mothers have lunch together back at home.'

'Is that so?'

'Yes, but can't get anything out of mother, she never gossips about the people from our village.'

'Ha, why would she? Most haven't left there in decades.'

'You're so right about that. I worked here a year, just enough to get me on the property ladder and commute here.'

'You're buying a place back home?'

'Yes, it's a derelict old farmhouse – you know, the one on the corner, where everybody thinks it's haunted because the man that sold the land only wanted the old farmhouse, built a wall around it, separated the land he sold, then collapsed and died. That's the story anyway and my guess is no one wants it because of the wall he died building. You know how superstitious everyone is there.'

'Yeah, I guess you're right about that. How come I didn't get the honour of meeting you before now?'

'Sophia, you walk around and never look at us and when you do, you shout at us, well to the target leaders anyways, screaming at us to all get our heads down and reach our targets. You're quite scary when you get like that.'

'Really, I don't mean to, it's just...'

'Enough already, we get it, don't we?' Allan interjects, sitting next to Jack, sitting here, in my place, with the ladies, sparing me the wrath of Rebecca's venomous tongue, hoping she won't press on with the heavy any longer.

'Oh look, my brother and his... wait, is that his girlfriend?'

Looking back from the table I see Adam arm in arm with a woman, her hair tied in a blonde bun, and quickly move my head back towards Jack. *Sweet Dreams* playing by Eurythmics through the surround. I blink at Allan and

Jack as Rebecca leaves the table in a hurry to meet her brother and his girlfriend.

'Another round, it's on me. Sophia what are you drinking?'

'Why Allan very kind, a double vodka please, straight up.'

'Wait let me get these, after all, I asked you all to come. Allan, you get the next round mate.'

'Well you got promoted Jack, congratulations again. I'll have a pint of beer please,' Clare interjects laughing as Jack stands up smiling at her.

'Same again Allan?'

'Yeah mate, yes please.'

'So, Sophia how long a holiday are you taking, going anywhere nice?'

'No just a week off, it's my birthday on Saturday. Going back to mother's, it's family thing.'

'Do you have any siblings?'

'Yes, a brother, you?'

'Yes, me too, I have a brother, up to no good mind you.'

'Ha, mine too. What kind of no good?'

'You know, a layabout good for nothing kind.'

'I know the feeling, mine is back-packing in Australia.'

'Sounds ominous.'

'quite the contrary really.'

'How so? Oh, I don't mean to pry, sorry.'

'No, it's totally fine, just taking a year or two. Oh, I don't know the nitty gritty Clare.'

'What do you think of Jerry?'

'Allan, he is my boss, that's all I think. What do you think about him?'

'A pertinent prick, if you ask me.'

I'm almost spitting my wine out as I laugh with my colleagues, never having time to see them as real human beings with characters of their own. I thought they just had to do the target deadlines and then clock off. I'm wondering how I'm going to approach my boyfriend with her. Do I make my announcement? Do I ask what the fuck he is doing over there? Do I just slip out the side entrance opposite me?

'Here we go, I got us all shots of Jager bombs. After three, 1, 2, 3 floor, cheers.'

'Ugh, that was disgusting,' I mutter.

'You obviously don't get out that often.'

'Clare, I work twelve-hour days, this is my real first night out in a couple of years.'

'Oh my gosh, no wonder you're always in a bad mood. We're going to have to change that, right, my round of shots, excuse me.'

Standing up so that she could go to the bar, I did it, without showing my face. No one over there knew it was me, sitting at my resident lunchtime table with
new friends, staring at the back wall. Rebecca plonks herself next to me, now cornered.

'Oh good, is that for me?' She necks her shot in one.

'Yup, that was for you,' I say wanting to hear what or who she just met, but not wanting to sound over keen.

'I've invited my brother over with his girlfriend. Mother is always saying women throw themselves at him, he is a bachelor you know.'

'Are they coming over here? The table isn't big enough.'

'It's okay. He said they were only having the one and going to dinner.'

'Dinner where?'

'Oh, he said The Ivy, why?'

'Oh, I meant, uh I totally forgot, I have dinner plans, in fact I'm late. Excuse me, it's been lovely, and we must do it again sometime. Bye guys, have fun, see you later.' Rebecca stands up with a perplexed look on her face with her drink in her hand. 'It is my 21st Saturday, will you come?'

I slide out of the open doors. 'Perhaps, see what I can do, bye.'

'Where is she going? I just got a round in.' I hear Jack as I hurriedly leave the side entrance. I head to my right up the next right-hand side street, walking as fast as I can home, via the back streets, through alleyways, hurrying eyes burning with tears in my eyes, stinging, blinking harder with each pace quickening.

Text from Jack: *Why did you leave, come back. Jack x.*

Me: *Sorry I double booked, I'm late for dinner. Sophia xx.*

I put a tick next to number 1) on my bucket list, putting a line through number 2) then circling it back in. Yes, date a lot, sod him, why is he taking her to bloody dinner? Should I dress under-dressed and spy on them? Wait, I'm already under-dressed! I bite my bottom lip as the shot hits my bloodstream, not thinking clearly yet again. A bachelor with women throwing themselves at him and me giving myself to him, ugh!

CHAPTER 12

✦✦✦✦

I rummage in the back of the wardrobes for my old fancy dress box that hasn't been opened since college; a black, long shiny wig with a fringe, a box of thick long fake eyelashes. I search frantically for the little tube of glue, pulling everything out one by one all over the floor. I tie my hair up with a pair of tights, putting the wig on in front of the mirror, sitting on the floor opposite the wardrobe door, sliding it so I can see, pulling it into position. Walking to the kitchen, I open a drawer looking for superglue, then return to the bedroom dresser opposite my bed, big round crystal lights down each side of the mirror. Holding an eyelash with tweezers, I add the glue, carefully placing the lashes on my left eye, then the right one, eyes watering, stinging. I try to pierce open my eyes, pulling my lower lids down not wanting my eyes to stick together, tears burning and running down the side of my nose and sides of my cheeks. I wait for three minutes, staring into the mirror and counting so the glue dries, trying not to blink. Picking out black hairclips from the box, I push them one by one onto the tights, keeping my wig steady in place, middle finger inside the corner of my eye, picking out a clump of eye-glue, then the other one, mouth open, scratching the sides of the wig, remembering how heavy it is. Looking through the wardrobe for some old gym jogging suits, I opt for a brown tracksuit quite burlesque. I put on my blue running shoes, tying the laces, looking at myself; *this is stupidly ridiculous, what on earth am I doing?* Looking out of the window, I see the night is drawing in, sun fading. I smile at the notion that by the time I walk up there they should have finished their dinner.

Taking off my gym suit, I opt for a knee-length black velvet dress and put my phone and keys in a black bag, smiling as I hurriedly run up the road, then start walking at a normal pace with a swagger I never had before. This is turning into prurience, but still I carry on. I need to watch and if necessary, follow them. If he drives off with her, I'll get an Uber to his house and try and see if they're on his terrace.

My phone beeps, making me jump, startling me in this pathetic state of mind. It keeps ringing and I just keep walking. then it rings again. I look at the number, not recognising it.

'Hello.'

'Hey stranger, how are you?'

'Hey Jules! I am, I'm really good thank you, long time.'

'I know, listen, I'm near yours, are you home?'

'Jules, I'm not at home and kind of busy at the moment. How long are you around for? Have you changed your number?'

'No, it's the same, you texted me your new address a couple of years ago. I'm here to see you silly, can you put me up for the night?'

'Ah, I got a new phone, didn't put all the numbers in. There's a spare key in the back garden, under the black pot near the privet, help yourself. I don't know what time I'll be back, soon though, okay?'

'See you soon. Where are you? I'll meet you if you're having a drink?'

'No, I'll be back shortly. Jules, I am doing something really stupid.'

'Tell please, what are you doing?'

'Spying on my boyfriend. He's in a restaurant with another woman, and I'm in disguise.'

'Ha, as what, a pumpkin?'

'Jules, am I doing the right thing?'

'Of course you bloody are. Cheeky sod, taking someone else out to dinner.'

'Wait, I see them leaving, I'll call you back, got to go, bye.'

I hang up the phone, hiding behind a tree trunk and watch them walk away from the Ivy, following a hundred feet behind. I look at my phone, pretending to text as I walk and look in their direction. I take a right turn up Warwick Avenue. The sky is turning dark and it's hard to see her properly behind a tree. I watch her lean in to kiss him. He pulls away, holding her arms, slightly pushing her backwards – it looks like trouble. I bite my bottom lip. Then I hear a door slam shut, and I'm startled to see a man appear from the house beside me.

'You okay love?'

'Yes just going home, good night.'

'Goodnight.'

I watch Adam going through a front door; I missed what just happened, what the fuck? Hiding with a racing heart, I wait for him to come out. I'm hoping he hurries up, or I'll go and bang on the door.

On my way home, I see a red Jaguar with Jack in the passenger seat. Jerry's car, why is Jack with him? Hmm. Picking up my pace now I run as fast as I can, heart pumping with adrenaline – the black wig starts to wobble loose. I pass the Ivy, placing my hand on the wig to keep it in place, and run as fast as I can. I'm looking forward to seeing my oldest, kindest friend. Turning the key, I see Jules dressed in denims, a white T-shirt with ebony straight hair, big blue eyes.

'You look dreadful, great disguise.'

'Can you tell it's me?'

'Did they see you? No, definitely not.'

'No.'

'Aw, come here you, give me a hug, suits you. I opened a bottle, drink?'

'Yeah, first let's do some vodka.'

'Spill the beans, come on.'

We stand in the kitchen, pouring vodka into two tumblers, necking the cool crisp liquid down in one. Then we pour more into our glasses, taking the bottle and tumblers into the bedroom. Julie brings the wine and glasses and we sit on the floor opposite the wardrobes. She pulls out a silver blonde straight bob wig and puts it on, sitting next to me and doing more shots of vodka. She listens to me whining on about my first night, crying as she leans onto my shoulders and looking at me with her big blue piercing eyes. She sticks her bottom lip out, listens to me moaning and sobbing my heart out, then stands up and walks out the door as I scream through a sob, 'What am I going to *do*?'

'I am going to get another bottle. You got another bottle of vodka right? If I am going to get you through this, we need more.'

'In the freezer, I think there's another one.'

She puts her phone on the iPod station, presses the silver button on the dresser, grabs a hairbrush and starts singing along into it with the Sugar Babes. She pulls me up to dance with her. I grab the hair straighteners and sing along, both of us swaying to the funky music, moving around the bedroom. Julie jumps on the bed, almost hitting her head on the moving fan. I crawl on the bed and stand up with her as we dance up and down and around to Rick James' *Super Freak* on full blast, arms swaying from left to right, both doing the same old routine. We get down off the bed, drinking wine now, and Jules changes into the old pumpkin dress, then she puts on Pinocchio and green tights.

Pulling my wig off; my hair still wrapped in tights, I change into lingerie and heels and we take it in turns dancing in the middle of the room, laughing at each another, falling onto the bed. *Hotel California* starts to play and I sit upright off the bed and stare into the mirror. I pull the tights off my head and my hair falls around as I turn to face Julie singing into the air and swaying from left to right. She's on the bed, swaying from side to side, and she stands up and hugs me as we raise our arms up at the same time and sing into the same hairbrush, shouting as loud as we can, thinking we sound like rock stars.

Some dance to remember, some dance to forget...

CHAPTER 13

✦✦✦✦

Waking with heavy eyes and nostalgic feelings, Jules can always be counted on to get into party mode. My mouth is dry. Wiping away the dry crustiness in the corners of my lips, head pounding, I sit up on the bed, still dressed in mixed lingerie and red stilettos. I look over. Sleeping beauty is fast asleep, snoring quietly with each slow breath, ebony hair covering the side of her face, her full lips ajar showing her white overbite. Getting up I slowly waddle to the kitchen, open the fridge door, bend to look in the fridge, grab a bottle of sparkling water, pour a glass, drink it in one, then pour another, but adding a dissolving pain tablet. I hear a loud yawn in the bedroom: 'Ah, help! I need some water, I am dying.'

'Okay I'm coming. Here, take this in your water –

wait, let the pain tablet settle before you drink it.'

'Ouch!'

'Me too, look at the mess. I'm going to start tidying to clear my head, where's my phone?'

'Don't know, leave it.'

'I need it.'

'You don't, you're on holiday remember.'

'Got it.'

Jules sits up drinking her medicinal water, pushing her hair around her ear, staring at her reflection in the mirror, mortified, gasping at herself. 'Oh, what the fuck am I wearing? Ha!'

'Phew, you're a bloody bad influence.'

'Are you going to take those dreadful eyelashes off yet?'

'I can't get them off.'

'Why not?'

'I used superglue.'

'You didn't! Ha...'

'Flaming hell, seven missed calls.'

'Off him? Let me look, has he sent you messages?'

'Wait, if you don't mind?'

Text from Adam: *Where are you, why aren't you answering my calls? Adam.*

'What's his excuse?'

'There isn't one.'

'What?'

'Don't respond.'

'I most definitely will not.'

'Where does all this stuff go, in that box?'

'Yup.'

'Okay, I am on it.'

'Jules there's fresh towels in the bathroom cupboard.'

'Okay thanks, but I think we should go out, get the tube somewhere, hang out like we use to.'

'Can't, got to go back home to the parents, they're flying out to Austin in a few days.'

'Oh yes, it's your birthday, how did I forget? I'll come back with you.'

'There's no need, honestly.'

'I'm coming with you.'

'Fine, I am taking a hot shower.'

My phone starts beeping. I ignore it, open the glass door and turn on the shower in the green mosaic patterned walls, biting my lip. I'm keen to see who's calling, and the phone continues ringing. I walk over to the free-standing sink, looking at the caller: private number. 'Leave a message.' I'm tutting to myself. I step into the hot jets, wipe my hair back with both hands underneath the water, trying to get the hot water to soften the glue, rubbing my eyes gently, trying to pry them off, nothing. I wash my hair, lathering with shampoo, washing the pain away from last night's shenanigans, stretching my arms up in the air, palms flat on the wall at the side of the silver shower, stretching my back to let the water fall with bubbles of soap. I wipe the condensation off with my left hand, seeing my ridiculous thick lashes reflected in the glass door and wish I hadn't seen them. I shake my head at myself for following them. 'What did you expect?'

'Who are you talking to?'

'Myself.'

'First sign of madness.'

'Ha ha, that ship sailed a long time ago, I'm afraid.'

'You said it. How long are you going to be?'

'Two minutes.'

'Okay hurry up, I need a pee.'

'One sec.'

Rubbing my eyes again I try one last time, this time a bit rougher. Patting myself dry, I wipe the mirror above the sink and see myself in the mirror. 'Oh bugger.'

'What's going on in there?'

'Look at my fucking face.'

'Oh, dearie me, makeup, I'll fix you, I think you're having an allergic reaction.'

'What, wouldn't I have had it last night?'

'Don't remember most of last night. Here, let's go sit in the bedroom, have you got any?'

'Any what?'

'You know those mm, hay fever things, histamines?'

'I don't suffer with hay fever, nor allergies.'

'I think you do now. Who's banging on your front door?'

'Oh shit, don't let him in.'

'Of course I won't, not after what he did to you.'

'Who are you?' she shouts.

'Who are *you*?' A man's voice.

'I asked you first, what do you want and who are you?'

'Is she in?'

'Maybe.'

'Sophia, are you going to talk to me, what have I done now?'

'Can you please shush? Why are you shouting? That's bloody rude.'

'Sorry, please can you get Sophia to come to the door instead of you, this is rather stupid.'

'Oh, is it?'

'I think so, yes.'

'Well she's busy, I'm afraid.'

'Busy doing what?'

'She is in the shower and I don't know you, so...'

'I am her....'

'Are you her partner?'

'Yes.'

'You weren't her partner last night. And you didn't hear it from me, but she knows about... you know.'

'Knows what exactly?'

'Last night, the blonde lady.'

'I can explain.'

'We both followed you with that pretty blonde.'

'You did what? It's not what you think.'

'Not what we saw, I'm afraid. There is nothing for

you here, I'm sorry, now please leave, she doesn't want to see you.'

'Fine, just tell her it wasn't what it looked like, I left within two minutes, if you'd both waited on your voyeuristic shenanigans! I am leaving you both to think about your actions and not waiting around. If you had waited, she would still be answering my calls.'

'Bye.'

'Do you believe him?'

'No way, absolutely not Sophia, do you? Forget him, look at the mess you were in last night, look at your face. Let me have a shower, I'll do your makeup, and if that doesn't work, we'll buy some allergy stuff along the way.'

CHAPTER 14

✦✦✦✦

Arriving at my parents, I see the familiar cars on the gravel, plus a silver Mercedes cabriolet. I bite my lip. Hmm, must have a visitor. Look down at my watch, 09.10am I sneak in, not wanting to be heard, softly dash up the mahogany spiral staircase on my right and straight into my room, sobbing. I leave the small gold suitcase next to the wall, stagger to my old bed and climb under the duvet with my thick lashes still stuck to my face.

My mother comes in. 'Happy birthday... oh my, what's wrong dear? Whoever did this to you, they will get their comeuppance, you'll see. Drink your tea, heard you sneak in. Drink it love, we're going to lunch later, you need to stop this nonsense, are you listening?'

'Fine, watch, here I'll drink your tea, I'll get up.'

I sit up, drinking tea, face wet through wiping my nose

with a tissue from the white shiny side cabinet, scented box of flowered pattern tissues. I look at my beautiful mother, short silver hair, wrinkles setting in, her small lips smiling at me, inset brown eyes, long lashes. I'm always thinking I was adopted, dad with his big blue bulging eyes, Austin looks like father and well, I just don't look like either. As a teenager I always teased mother and father that I was the milkman's, wondering where my big brown eyes came from. Mother insisted they're from her father. I didn't get to know him, he passed away when I was a baby, mum said. No family photographs – lost when mum and dad moved with me as a toddler from London to the country. Dad blames the removal men for losing his golf clubs too. Dad tried to take them to court, but the removal company went into liquidation. I scratch my eyes at the side temples, pulling at the lashes.

'Don't love, they'll come off soon enough, and your face is red enough from all that sobbing. What's wrong dear? It's obviously a man.'

'Mother I'll freshen up, see you downstairs and thank you for the tea.'

'Okay, see you downstairs.'

'Mum?'

'Yes?'

'Where are we having lunch?'

'Your favourite.'

'Perfect.'

'Mother...'

'Yes?'

'Thank you.'

'See you shortly.' Mother closes the door; I can hear her walking downstairs.

'She's getting up Frank.'

'What's wrong with her, you told her about...?'

'She won't say love, I think it's man trouble.' I get out of bed and walk out of the door. I stand at the top of the huge mahogany banister, seeing the chandelier crystal lights glow. As I lean on the banister I see my parents standing an inch away from each other at the bottom of the spiral staircase.

'Guys I can hear you, told me what?'

'Ha, you're alive! Are you joining us love?'

'Dad I'll be down soon, okay?'

'Happy birthday, and hurry up, we got you a gift, you will love it.'

'Yeah, I know, I'll be down soon, okay.'

I unpack my gold suitcase, biting my lips, and unfold my clothes, putting them in an old wooden antique wardrobe mother must have picked up somewhere. I hang my clothes on wooden coat hangers and take my wash bag out of the case. I open the brown door and walk into the modern white bathroom, looking into the cupboards in the hope that mother has stocked them with my creams. Bare cupboards, only three white fluffy towels on the other side. 'Mum?'

I dress in a black jogging suite, white T-shirt and a big

cream woolly sweater. I'm freezing in this massive open-aired house, only one floor at the top, a huge hallway with six bedrooms, two opposites, facing from one side of the massive hallway. Why on earth have they got six bloody rooms? Shaking my head, I casually walk down the spiral staircase, looking up at the chandelier on my way down and smiling at the lilies centre stage. I walk through the huge hallway towards the back of the house.

'Come and sit down next to your father.'

'What's up, are you in trouble?'

'Dad, no.'

'She won't tell you anyway Frank, you know what she's like.'

'Yes, she gets that from you. Have you heard what happened to that poor woman on the news, that boss of yours, did he hurt you? Looks and sounds bloody guilty to me.'

'What is on the news?'

'Is that why you're so upset love, did you know her? Look, if you're in trouble or if anyone hurt you, I'll get the best barrister.'

'What, dad?'

'Shh, what? Mother no I didn't know her, well I did in a sort of manner... oh my gosh, that happened last night?'

The 72-inch black TV blares through the speakers: 'Late last night Lucy Cunningham, who is married to the entrepreneur Jerry Cunningham, was strangled in her home. Police say they are appealing for any witnesses. Here is a statement from her husband: 'We just renewed our vows a couple of months ago. If anyone knows anything please, please come forward.'

Dad pauses the TV with the remote.

'Looks guilty to me. That's your boss, is that why you're upset?'

'You can speak to us dear. Did you know about this?'

'What's with all the questions guys?'

'Clearly something's up with you, I want to know.'

'Dad leave it, it's nothing to do with that, it's not that at all.'

CHAPTER 15

✦✦✦✦

I'm smiling with the highlights earlier this morning. I'm happy in the notion that finally he was arrested, having heard it on the radio: 'Mr Jerry Cunningham, Mrs Cunningham's husband, aged 53 years, has been arrested on suspicion of murdering Mrs Lucy Cunningham, aged 32'.

A very serious crime, knowing it's Jerry. Did Sophia and her crazy friend know something? Perhaps she's a tad crazy, but she isn't capable of something like that. How am I going to go after Jerry, how am I going to prove it was him? How am I going to prove it wasn't me, more to the point? The bastard. As the last man to see her, I could be framed for her murder.

Dressed in casual attire, denims and a black T-shirt, I walk out to the room next door, open the white vinyl triple doors, take out the dry cleaning, grab some plastic pressed black trousers and pull out a small black suitcase. I add two grey cashmere sweaters and two blue ones, two white shirts, two pairs of denims, two pairs of brown and black leather shoes, two pairs of black socks and three black Armani boxer shorts, reminding myself to leave a note for the cleaner. I walk down the hallway and into the grey and white tiled kitchen, leaning over the middle tower, writing. *Gone out, please just do bedroom and main bathroom, it's all clean from Wednesday, many thanks. Adam.*

I head out to the cars, opting for the Porsche. The sun is shining outside, suggesting another hot day, so I'm not too fussed. I put my suitcase in the boot and get in, pressing for the roof. I set off towards the M4, thinking about Rebecca's birthday. Every bloody year she has to make such a fuss. Normally I work, it's been five years, so this time I decided to show my face when Rebecca insisted the other night that I had to come along at the Bell.

Driving past her house, I see the blinds are closed and hope she is okay, then realising her birthday is today. I pull over and dial the florist's number, then hang up, realising she said she was going to her mother's. What if she changed her mind? I drive off, realising there isn't much I can do. She won't accept anything from me, they'll go straight in the bin, that much I do know! I zoom off thinking about seeing the family, a totally dysfunctional one at that. Rebecca the alcoholic little sister, while her older sister Rachel lives on a farm with her partner, addicted to buying horses, nine of them and counting. I wish it was her bloody birthday – at least I could add to her collection. Andrew, my younger brother, still older than the two spoilt brats. Andrew is living off mother in a small flat in Clapham Junction, working in a bar, for Christ's sakes. He's considering going to Cambridge, and for what? About bloody time he did something with his life, and I'll tell him when I get the chance of us walking the estate, alone later.

Phone starts ringing through surround; what would you like to do, say yes to answer or no to end the call?

'Yes?'

'Hello.'

'Hello, are you coming later, you haven't forgotten, have you?'

'Hello mum, already set off.'

'Oh, what a nice surprise, will you be here for brunch?'

'Yes mum.'

'Oh, your sister hasn't got up yet, nobody's here yet.'

'Okay mum, I'll be there in an hour.'

'That will be 10.30. Did you know Andrew has a place at Saint James darling?'

'Really? That's brilliant.'

'Bye love.'

'Bye mum.' The phone went silent before she heard me laugh.

CHAPTER 16

✦✦✦✦

'Ah to hell with the commotion, your present is here love, happy birthday.' I open a purple box, and inside is a black car key with a silver Mercedes sign on it. I'm laughing and smiling back at my parents in disbelief.

'Oh my gosh, is that mine outside? Come on, I love it thanks mum, dad, I haven't driven since my test.'

'You will be later love, got you a fresh hour's lesson. Let's take her out for a spin.'

'Mum, dad, I love you both so much, thank you so much.' I hug them both under the oval archway, fling the doors open and hurriedly walk over to the shining Mercedes – my new independence!

'Get in then.'

'Okay, sit in with me, can we drive around here?'

Dad has already pressed the button to make the

electric roof slide back above our heads. Mother is standing smiling underneath the arch of the doors in her silk grey dressing gown, hair in small pink curlers, in a net from last night. Always well kept. Dad giving me a lecture as per, 'It's automatic, so you only use your hands for the steering wheel, use one foot, that's the brake and that's the...'

'Dad I know, mum gave me lessons and I did pass my test you know!'

'Yeah but it's been years. Let's take it for a spin, drive down the road, mirror signal manoeuvre, seatbelts, press the button.'

'Where is the button?' I whisper overzealously.

'Calm down, no rush, familiarise yourself with all the buttons love.'

'There's too many, what's this one?'

'The roof, don't press it.'

'Okay'. I beam at dad, then look at the black oval in the hole and press a button to release the handbrake. Slowly we set off down the shingle driveway through the gold electric gates, driving like a snail down the road.

'A bit faster love, bloody hell!'

'Dad!'

'You're doing five miles an hour love, put your bloody foot down.'

'You got it.'

I speed off down the road, hitting 34mph, revving the accelerator. Dad's holding onto the side of his door screaming at me, 'The brake, hit the brake, slow down!'

'But you said... ugh, I'm scared to put my foot on it.'

'Take your foot off the accelerator and press the brake, gentle, not too hard.'

'Er, right.'

I press the brake as gently as I can with my right foot, slowing down, then push my foot harder in a panic and come to a halt, the tyres screeching on the tarmac, rubber smelling inside the car. Dad gets out, wiping his brow, big beer belly popping out of his brown dressing gown, black hairy chest bare, his blue boxer shorts. With his skinny white legs and his brown slippers, he walks in front of the car, his arms in the air, black short hair still messy from last night. He wipes the top of his hair, blowing in the wind.

'I'm driving home, that's enough till your lesson later. Get out, come on',

'Fine, you said speed up dad.'

'Yes, but bloody hell, you could have killed us.'

'Stop exaggerating.'

'You're going to love this Merc when you can actually drive.'

'Told you for years I didn't need a car dad, not where I live, but I love it so much, thank you.' I lean over to kiss the side of his face as he drives back down the road. I take in the beauty of all the oak trees and look at our huge house in the distance. The gates open and we pull in, but I'm looking at a police car. My eyes are open wide and I bite my lips together. Mother is inviting them in, offering them biscuits and tea, probably with her best china.

'What the hell! If it's Austin, I'm going straight there,' says dad.

'You're going in the next week, aren't you?'

'Yes, but your bloody brother is causing us so much bloody grief.'

'What's he done now?' he asks in the lightly aired hallway smelling of the fresh lilies on the white marble tower. I'm trying to escape my thoughts, sighing *this is it, it's me, not my brother. Mum and dad are going to go berserk.*

'What's going on, is it Austin?' asks dad. 'Is he all right, what's he done now? Has he done a runner from that?'

'Frank, it's not Austin this time.'

Mother nods in my direction, and dad looks at me in shock and disgust. The two officers, both female, are looking at me as well, all four-staring back at me. I wipe my hair around my right ear, bite my lip, eyes wide open looking back at them, *I'm wondering what the fuck I am going to tell them?*

'What has she done?'

'Dad.'

'Sophia Evans?'

'Yes?'

'You have the right to remain silent, anything you do say will be evidence in the court of law, you have the right to...' The words mumble in my head as the cold handcuffs tight on my wrists.

'What, no, what are you doing, get these off me, now, mum, dad help me, please? It's my birthday. What are you doing, why, get off me. Ouch, they're hurting my wrists.'

'What has she done?' Dad screams.

Now I'm being dragged by the officer's my head-first into the back of the police car with an officer in the back with me.

My parents' faces are sullen under the wide-open archway doors, mum with her hand over her mouth and my dad looks at me like he never did before. Dad runs at the gates shouting as I turn my head around. I cry loudly, looking at my mother's sad face and dad losing his dignity with all and sundry running after the car.

'Don't worry love I'll get you the best lawyer, you hear me love?'

CHAPTER 17

✦✦✦✦

The marquee is being erected, and there are raindrops on the windows. I'm watching people walk round the neatly-cut grass, taking in the beauty. The double doors open into the hall, luxurious red carpet rolling outside to the marquee, workmen with black and white shirts advertising the company, 'Marquees R Us.' I smile at mother dashing around the huge white vinyl kitchen, silver handles, opening cupboards, prepping brunch, dashing from kitchen to dining room, setting the table for five people, best silverware, napkins. She's holding her phone: 'Hurry up dear, Adam's here, brunch is in half an hour, will you be here?'

Rebecca walks through the hallway, rubbing her eyes, long brunette wavy bedhead hair, white pyjamas, white linen robe, face sullen, knowing she isn't allowed to open her presents until later. Mother always made us wait until late, ensuring everybody's there, especially on an important birthday. I walk straight past the massive round breakfast table, not even looking at the silver twenty-first stand, edible cake and glitter that mother gave me carry to the table earlier, placing it carefully in the centre. We all got one and now it's my little sister's turn to reach 21. I'm thinking 'ungrateful cow' as I watch her walk over to the fridge and open a bottle of water. She's drinking straight out of the bottle, not even realising my presence, or if she has, she hasn't let on. I'm standing by the window looking at tables being positioned under the white roof, chairs being carried, people cleaning windows, silverware being polished, everyone running around the grounds like clockwork toys.

'Good morning sis, late for brunch, couldn't miss mother's birthday feasts, could I? I'll take you out afterwards, let's go buy you something, what would you like?'

'It's my 21st, can I have anything?'

'It isn't actually your birthday yet, you don't change do you! What do you want?'

'Oh, I don't know. Wow, mum, the table! It's so pretty, thank you.'

Rebecca kisses mother and me on the cheek, huge eyes shining, smiling whilst stretching her shoulders, waking up, nodding approval that it's her turn to be spoilt.

Rebecca missed her 18th, spending it in the Priory

recovering from alcoholism. She'd been found in a ditch the day before, half a mile from here. A neighbour walking her dog rang an ambulance, knowing she was unconscious, waited until they arrived, then walked to tell mother the news. The next day mother drove her to the Priory herself, and made her stay in there without embarrassment. She had to cancel all the work staff, stored the cake in a cupboard, telephoned everybody telling us all about her youngest daughter. She was gossiping to the neighbours like it was normal and now her turn to have a member of the family in a rehabilitation centre. I was full of contempt, knowing that everyone knew and mother sounding proud. I didn't know if she did what she did as a sigh of relief or an ambivalent moment in getting help for her. Did she really have a problem or was she merely doing what most teenagers do? Mother was always repeating on the phone for years: 'she comes home drunk every night, drinks in the mornings, thank god she's okay now.'

Three times in the last five years she has been in and out. Third time lucky, she seems to be coping, not drinking as much, though she still likes to party and has a drink like the rest. I'm hoping my little sis has it under control and wondering if mother over-reacted.

Andrew walks in, wearing a black and white tuxedo. Short mousy brown hair, brown inset eyes, grinning with his pearly, straight, white teeth. He's holding hands with a tall skinny blonde; huge blue eyes, dressed in a short black halter neck dress, black heels, holding onto his arm. He blurts out, 'We're married.' Mother turns around and drops the white china onto the ground, smashing it into pieces, Rebecca looks at me and I stare at her. I help mother to pick up the pieces. Rebecca holds onto Andrew, kissing him, pulling his new bride down onto a chair.

'Tell us everything, come on!'

Mother and I walk back into the airy kitchen and throw the china into the automatic silver bin. She's holding back her tears, not wanting to turn around, her blue eyes, turning darker, looking at me.

'I'm not happy.'

'It's happened.'

'Why has he done this? I don't even know her.'

'Mother, that's probably why he did it.'

'What do you mean son?'

'I mean that perhaps you wouldn't have approved of her.'

'Absolutely not dear. I need to reset the table for six people.'

'Come on, let's do it together.'

'Andrew, please introduce us?'

'Mother this is Sally, Sally this is my mother, Mary.'

Sally sits still, then stands up smiling at mother, shaking her hand, shyly meeting mother's gaze. Mother stands over Andrew, watching her sitting back down, crossing her tanned skinny legs.

'Are you hungry, Sally?'

'Parched, Mary.'

'Ha, Sally! You will fit right into this family.'

'Rebecca, if you don't mind?'

'Come on mum, its good news, he finally has a woman. You always walk around shouting 'when are these two going to finally settle?'

'Rebecca, that's enough, go and change for brunch. As you can see, we're all waiting for you.'

'Fine, five minutes.'

Mother pours the tea from the silver jug. 'When, where and...?'

'Just now at the town hall, we got the 10am slot, booked it a week ago.'

'A week ago? How long have you been courting?'

'Mother, Sally is a personal assistant at Saint James.'

'Oh, jolly good. How do you like it there, are you fitting in son?'

'Seems I am.'

'Andrew, this is rather short notice, how do we celebrate your marriage?'

'Mother just let's have a reception here today, make it a double celebration, and it's not her actual birthday today anyway. Reception and birthday, right here, all my Uni friends are coming, my friends from Clapham and the bar.'

'What about you dear?'

'My family are in Hawaii, they live there, but my friends from work are coming too, if that's okay?'

'Oh, I do wish to meet your acquaintances from Saint James, the pair of you.'

As mother gets out of her seat and walks back towards the bacon sizzling under the grill, Andrew's whispering in her ear. 'See, I told you she would like you.'

Sally leans in, kissing my brother full on the lips as mother, barely concealing her contempt, places a silver tray with jugs of fresh orange, grapefruit and apple juices rather noisily on the table.

Rebecca flounces back in dressed in a short, yellow summer dress, smiling. She sits next to her new playmate and picks up the jar of apple juice, whilst mother comes back over and places hot plates one at a time in front of us.

'Let's eat.' We all tuck into a traditional full English brunch, two slices of bacon, one sausage and two poached eggs each, fresh bread neatly sliced, still warm from the baker dropping it off earlier. I'm holding onto a slice of bread and wondering what mother must be thinking.

CHAPTER 18

✦✦✦✦

DC Williams and Detective Sergeant Jeffery sit across a blue plastic table separating us, both in uniforms, stern looks catching my gaze. 'Interview commencing 10.24am Saturday 9th August 2019.'

'Sophia Evans.'

'Yes?'

'Where were you last night?'

'I, uh, was watching my, uh… spying on my partner.' I scratch my head, twisting curls around my ear, fidgeting, putting my hands under my thighs, posture straight.

'Can you tell us what you saw?'

'I was in disguise. I followed them to Warwick Avenue, and I saw her try to kiss him. I hid behind a tree, trying to see. He pulled away from her and held her arms back, he didn't kiss her, I know that much. I saw Jerry and Jack drive past on my way back home.'

'What happened after that?'

'Do I need a solicitor?'

'Do you want a solicitor? And who is Jack?'

'I haven't committed a crime so no, I don't need one. He works for Jerry, got a promotion, he starts on Monday. Oh my god, is Jack dead too?'

'Julie Jackson is in custody, and we need to eliminate you both from suspicion of the crime.'

'What has she been arrested for?'

'We need to establish everything.'

I bite my lip, thinking about poor Jules.

'You said in your statement earlier you got home at 10.05 and she was already in your house waiting for you.'

'That is correct.'

'Like I said, we have to go over everything and check both of your statements out.'

'How did you find her?'

'We telephoned her; she is here being interviewed. This is a murder case, nonetheless you two have a long way to go until we find out the truth.'

'You know it wasn't me, why would Jules do anything? She doesn't know any of them, I really don't understand what the hell is going on any more.'

'Why don't you understand?'

'I don't understand why you arrested a woman that

visited me, wasn't in the vicinity, nowhere near the Ivy, nowhere near the scene of the horrid crime.'

'Were you?'

'Was I what?'

'At the scene?'

An officer walks inside and nods over. DC Williams and DS Jeffery's faces are stern.

'Interview terminated 10.34.' He presses the black box and they both walk out of the room, slam the thick brown solid door. I sigh out loud and rest my head in my hands, elbows on the table.

The door opens and DS Jeffery beckons with a curly finger.

'You're free to go.'

'Jules too?'

'We are taking you back separately.'

'What about Jack, is he ok?'

'Come on, haven't got all day, I'm afraid I cannot discuss anything with you.'

'I'll call Jack.'

'No you won't, he's a suspect now, no contact. Sign here, read all of this first and then sign it.'

CHAPTER 19

✦✦✦✦

'What are you going to order, sis?'

'Wine please, Adam.'

'Not a chance.'

'Why on earth not?'

'Because I said so.'

'It's my birthday.'

'Fine Becca, but just half a glass, you're driving, remember.'

'Dad would have been proud of you, you know.'

'Do you think so?'

'Yes, I really think so.'

'Well I followed in his footsteps. It was all I wanted to do when he died.'

'Ads, you were born to do your job, the word is you are the best, just like dad was.'

'Becca, is that why you went off the rails?'

'I don't know, I was only 11, I started then.'

'Started what?'

'You know.'

'You started drinking at 11? Fuck sake sis!'

'Well nobody had any time for me, you had left home, nowhere to be seen, Andrew was at Uni and Rachel went to live with Sam, and I... well, I was left with mum constantly crying in her room, she never came out.'

'Ah, that's why you were so terrible at school, I get it now. What do you want to do with your life?'

'Mum gave me twenty thousand and I'm buying that house on the corner of the old farm, that one nobody wants, do you know where I mean?'

'Yes, why that one, how much is it?'

'It's on the market at two hundred and twenty.'

'How will you afford the mortgage?'

'I have a career, I'll commute, do it up. Mum will help me, you know how she loves to interfere, especially with projects.'

'I would like to discuss your career.'

'What about it?'

'I don't want you working there.'

'Why not?'

'It's not a permanent career.'

'Is so.'

'Becca, it isn't, the company is going to go bust.'

'How so?'

'Trust me.'

'Well what will I do? The sale is almost finalised. What is going on, how can a company like that go bust? It's the best in London, it's a success and I like my job.'

'Do you listen to or watch the news?'

'Not much, I am too busy.'

'Too busy doing what exactly?'

'Meeting friends, looking at furniture, working really hard, that kind of busy.'

'You ought to pay more attention to things.'

'Like what?'

'The news!'

'Why?'

'Ugh, what are you eating?'

'Shall we share a pesto pizza?'

'Yes, order me a pint, going for a piss.'

'You're driving, remember?' Becca smiles up at her brother.

'OK Becca.' I leave the table, passing people chatting, kids laugh out loud, babies cry. I look at the table on my right, I see her sitting opposite a woman, notice her curly bob, look at her slender neck, light blue straps on her shoulders, smile at the older lady, looking back at me. I'd recognise her anywhere. I know the older woman but can't think from where. I conjure up the courage to go over and ask is she okay, is she having a nice birthday? Nah, just walk back past without a second glance, don't be so stupid, she despises you, remember?

I sit back down and drink the pint in one, thinking how pretty she looked, even from the back. The pesto pizza arrives, Becca sips her spritzer.

'Adam, I'm a tad thirsty?'

'Yes.' Becca, yes.'

'Another?'

'Becca, yes.'

'Are you all right?' Becca leans over closer.

'Yes, no, yes, I'm having another pint.'

'What's wrong?'

'Your boss is back there.'

'Sophia Evans?'

'Yes.'

'And that has a reference to you, why?'

'It's complicated.'

'Is that why you don't want me to work for her?'

'No, it's not that at all, it's just...'

'Oh, please spill!'

'Becca, can we just eat and leave please?'

'Sure.'

'Hurry up then.'

'Why, what's the big deal?'

'We were dating.'

'When?'

'That's irrelevant.'

'I think it's very relevant, I thought you were dating that tall blonde from last week.'

'That's why it's complicated.'

'How so?'

'Finished? I'll leave fifty quid on the table, come on, we're leaving.'

'Fine.'

'See you at home. Where are you going now?'

'To show off my new car before the party starts.'

'See you later sis, drive safely.'

'Love you.'

'Love you too, bye.' Now I'm sitting in my Porsche with the roof up, sweating; hitting the AC on full, watching the Express, hoping to catch a glimpse of her, wanting to go straight over, wanting to make it all okay, take her out for her birthday, spoil her. I'm thinking of all the things I can tell her, then realising that I'd be breaking the law, talking to a suspect. I still want to try and say something, anything...

CHAPTER 20

✦✦✦✦

Lots of cars are piled up, covering the side pathways towards the estate; not being able to drive into the grounds, we park at the back, on a country lane.

'How many has she invited?'

'It's a twenty-first, I expect there'll be a lot of young people here.'

'Please remind me, why we are here?'

'I said we would show our faces, it's rude not to.'

'Fine but I don't know them. I have no idea why you would say yes to a stranger.'

'Come on, I have known Mary for donkeys' years, you used to go to nursery with Andrew.'

'Who is Andrew?'

'A suitor.'

'Dad, turn around, I want to leave, now dad!'

'Hang on love, let's just show our faces, have a drink and go out to dinner, right?'

'Fine, but mother don't you dare interfere with this Andrew person.'

'As you wish love.' We walk up the lane, towards the pretty white cottages, and the dusty lane in the dry heat makes my black heels scuff at each step. I'm wearing a pastel blue knee-length, straps over my shoulders. *I just want dad to get into a mood and turn around.* We're greeted by a waiter holding a silver tray of champagne. I take one and drink it in one, then put it back on the tray and take another.

'Sophia! Must you?'

'You brought us here to this silly twenty-first, and you're trying to set me up.'

'Oh, look, Andrew! Hi, hello we're here, there he is love.'

'Hello.'

'Hello, I'm Sophia.'

'You haven't changed a bit, how are you? This is my wife Sally, meet Sophia.'

'Nice to meet you Sally.'

'You too Sophia, how do you two know each other?'

'We went to nursery apparently, my mother just informed me. We had au pairs back then in the good old days. Lovely to see you again.'

'Yes, the good old days indeed, good to see you again, have fun.'

'You too, see you later.' I stand still watching mum and dad over the other side talk to a woman I assume is Rebecca's mother. I wish someone would walk past with more champagne. My black Jimmy Choo heels are digging into the neatly cut grass, slowly going down into the ground. Wishing it would swallow me right up. Everyone is dressed in summer ball gowns, hair neatly done and smelling of spray and perfume, perfect twenty-year-old and some, make-up perfect. Some people walk past laughing with flutes in their hands, then Rebecca runs towards me, dressed in a tight pastel-purple lace-embroidered dress with a bottle in her hand.

'You made it! I didn't think you would come, drink?'

'Yummy, yes please I am parched.'

'Ha, love it. Adam saw you earlier in Express, we were in there, is the company going bust?'

'Uh, not sure.'

'You would tell me, wouldn't you?'

'Yes. Is your brother here?'

'Yes, in fact I wouldn't turn around, he's behind you. Don't worry, way behind us, under the marquee. He said you two dated, is that right?'

'He's watching us?'

'Yup.'

'Oh bugger.'

'What's up with you two? You're both acting really weird.'

'It's complicated.'

'That's what he said. You're perfect together if you want my opinion. Eh, he's coming over, shall I fill your glass up quick here? Have fun.'

'Yeah, thank you. Rebecca?'

'Yes?'

'Thank you, and happy birthday.'

'Thank you, have fun.' Why is this family all about saying have fun? I don't want to turn around, but I feel the presence of him behind me and his breath on my neck gives me goosebumps as he slowly appears at my side, taking my hand. Precariously I pull it away, not wanting to look at him. Too late. He is standing in front of me staring into my eyes. My eyes are transfixed by his.

'You look amazing.'

'Adam, I honestly don't know what to say to you.'

'Then don't say anything, just stand here.'

'I can't move, my heels are stuck!'

'You're always a damsel in distress.'

'I certainly am not, thank you very much.'

'You are when you're in my company.'

'I'm here with my parents, they know your mother, I had no idea.'

'I'm glad you had no idea.'

'Why is that?'

'Must I state the obvious?'

'No.'

'You're a star, you know that. How many have you had? Take a walk with me please.'

'Where?'

'Somewhere private.'

'I don't think we should.'

'I have to speak to you Sophia, it's very important. Mother rents out the cottages there, see? Hence all the guests. Mine's the cottage over there, it's totally private. We must talk, come on.'

'Fine, but Adam I really need to know why you had your arms linked together again, and why go inside her home. What time did you leave, did you kiss her inside her house, what happened?'

'I didn't do it, trust me, I'm being set up. I got a call earlier from someone on the inside. I know you were arrested earlier, what did you say?'

'Mother and father are expecting me, we're going to dinner soon. Isn't this illegal?'

'You're a suspect, as am I. Remember when I had my sweater in Nobu?'

'Yes, you didn't have it afterwards, did Jerry take it?'

'That's why I'm asking you, did you see him take it? I know, so I'm going to be framed with this.'

'Why did you go into her house?'

'She was afraid to be left alone, said that Jerry would see to her. I left after two minutes, just made sure she got in safely.'

'None of this makes sense. Jack was in Jerry's car, they drove past me, after I saw you go into her home.'

'What? Who's Jack? And I need to tell you, I'm completely in love with you.'

'Why are you saying this?'

'Sophia, you're the one for me, I love you. From the first day you had the newspaper stuck to your face months ago, it is and always will be you.'

'I... uh...'

'Shh, kiss me.' He kisses me softly, arms wrapped around my waist, pulling me up into him, pushing me backwards, holding my shoulders with his hands, firm, staring into my eyes, winking at me.

'Let's get out of here.'

'Where?'

'It's your birthday. Now I have you with me, I would like to take you out.'

'We *are* out. It's your sister's party, we cannot just leave.'

'Sure, we can, come on, we're going, leaving. My car is parked on the lane, hold my hand. Ready?'

'Ready.'

Adam guides me past the marquee on our right, walking on cobbles past everybody dancing, people moving in and out of the doors from the hall to the garden, peering over at where mother was earlier, seeing dad watching me hand in hand, touching my mother's shoulder. They turn around, mother and father watch us head out past two waiters standing by the silver gates holding trays of champagne. Two more replace them with full trays and the other two inside back towards the hallway.

CHAPTER 21

✦✦✦✦

Adam opens the passenger door and I demurely put my ankles together, sitting in, feet and legs together, looking straight ahead. Mother and father are standing at the entrance smiling, dad holding mother's hand and watching with approval. I bite my bottom lip, stare at them.

'Where are we going?'

'It's a surprise. Wouldn't be a proper birthday now would it, if I told you?'

'A surprise in this small village, you cannot be serious!'

'What do you want for your birthday?'

'Nothing really, I'm a low-key kind of girl.'

'Come on, must be something, what did you get from your parents?'

'That car there.'

'Nice, didn't know you drove.'

'Ha.'

'Why are you laughing?'

'Cos you had way too many to drive your parents back home.'

'No, dad drove us.'

'Good, they're not stranded then.'

'Dad doesn't drink, knows mother and I like our....'

'I saw you earlier.'

'Rebecca said.'

'Gosh, that girl.'

'Said we're perfect together.'

'Is that so?'

'Asked why we were acting really weird.'

'Are we?'

'What?'

'Really weird.'

'I guess so.'

'What did my sister say?'

'Asked if the company is going bust. I said it's complicated, she said that you said the same when she prompted you with questions about me. What did you tell her about me?'

'I said we were dating. I need to use my phone, one sec.'

'Adam, why are we pulling into here?'

'You'll see.'

'It's an airfield.'

'Are you scared?' Adam taps away on his phone.

'Of what?'

'Flying.'

'Not at all.'

'Good, cos you're flying the plane.'

'What?'

'Ha, only joking, we're going to fly that black jet there, see?'

'Which one?'

'The third on the left, see?'

'Oh my gosh, it's tiny, who is the pilot?'

'Ha, come on.' He opens my door, takes my hand. The electric doors open and the black and white stairs start unfolding onto the tarmac. Three windows blacked out on the side of the jet. Adam holds my hand as I go up first. My dress blows in the wind, tight round my waist, fitted tightly around my breasts. Two straps hold my dress in place. My stomach starts churning and I smell the leather as I step into the cool air inside. I sit on a cream leather seat watching him pressing buttons in the cockpit, scratching my head.

'Come sit here, put your belt on, you can put the headset on if you want to.'

'Okay.'

'Just for take-off, listen to air traffic control. You can take them off once we're up in the air.'

'Okay. Where are we flying to?'

'Not that far.'

'How do you know how to fly?'

'My dad taught me. Shh, ready?'

'Ready, oh my gosh!' I watch him listening to air traffic control, heading towards a tiny runway. I wipe my hair round the headset, staring ahead. We're speeding up and he pulls on the controls.

'We're travelling at 200 mph, ready?'

'Yes.' I look down onto the ground out of the window. The sun is shining from a cloudless sky over little cars, like dots on the streets.

'Fifteen thousand feet. Amazing, right?'

'Wow, thank you, this is the best birthday ever.'

'We got all day and night.'

'We're flying all day and night?'

'You have got your passport on you, right?'

'Adam, no.'

'London?'

'Sounds good to me, how long until we...'

'Twenty minutes.'

'Wow.'

'We're going to start descending; do you want to put your headset on?'

'No, I trust you.'

'Finally.'

'Adam, I knew it wasn't you.'

'Enough darling, it's your day, let's just enjoy, okay?'

'Sure.' We land at London City airport, and a black chauffeur in a top hat awaits us at the side of the plane.

He opens our doors one at a time, and we sit next to each other on the black leather.

'Where to sir?' asks the chauffeur.

'Londrino restaurant SE1.' He turns to me. 'Hungry?'

'Yes.'

'Good. It's a pretty wine bar too, you'll love it.'

'Thank you.'

Adam orders champagne and I sit there watching him watching me, smiling at me, his right elbow on the white linen, his white shirt partly unbuttoned and baring his olive chest, denims fitted to perfection.

'Wait here, I'll be back soon, okay?'

'Where are you going?'

'To see a friend next door.'

'Okay.'

'Order for me.'

'What would you like?'

'Seafood. Figure it out, I'll be back soon.' He gets up, kisses me on my forehead, walks out of the doors. I scratch my head and bite my lip, sipping the bubbles. Not sure I have ever been left at a dinner table on a date before, unless they did a moonlight flit.

'Would you like to order, or wait until he comes back?'

'Yes, I'll have the sea bass please, and the lobster in ginger, with king prawns please.'

'Any olives whilst you wait?'

'Yes please.'

'Coming up. Water?

'Oh, yes.'

'Still or sparkling?'

'Sparkling and a bottle of still please.' I look at my watch: 17.20pm. The days flying by. I rub my eyes and sit sipping the crisp champagne on my palate and eat an olive as demurely as possible.

Adam walks back in, and I look at my watch, 18.15pm.

'You're timing me?'

'You've been gone ages.'

'Adam what are you doing?' He's down on one knee. Everybody stops talking and someone taps their glass. I hear in the distance: 'Sophia will you do me the honour of becoming my wife?' My mouth falls wide open and I stare at him smiling up at me, looking quite nervous. His smile turns and he closes his mouth, sweat on his brow, and smiles back at me, I stare down at his hand; it's shaking. He's holding a massive shiny diamond in a cream box.

'Well?'

'Huh... yes.'

'She said yes!' He puts the ring on my finger and leans up to kiss me, and I bend down to meet his lips. Everybody starts clapping and cheering. Adam stands up, pulling me up to him, and stands facing everyone. He grabs me softly and kisses me. Everybody is still cheering – it's a standing ovation.

'Where did you get this? It's so pretty.'

'Alex Monroe, next door.'

'You planned this?'

'It was unexpected, I'm just happy you will be my wife. I'm irrevocably in love with you.'

'I love you too.'

'Cheers.'

'Cheers Sophia, I so bloody love you, I have ever since the first day I saw you in the Bell, like I said earlier.'

Back at the party, everyone's dancing to the music in the humid summer night air and twenty to midnight. Adam brings over a bottle of champagne, pours me a flute, pours himself one, downs it in one and pours himself another. We're sitting outside his little cottage around a white table and chairs, mother, father and Liz nowhere in sight. Only about fifty people are left dancing away to 80's and 90s music by the DJ. Then I hear a noise.

'Hear that?'

'What the fuck, sirens! Why here, why now?'

'I got to go.'

'You're innocent, why are you running away?'

'I'll stay and face it. Jerry must have placed my sweater somewhere, look go back into work, seduce him.'

'I beg your pardon?'

'Find out everything Sophia, you're smart.'

'But...'

'Shh, kiss me.' He puts his hands softly around my

neck, pulling me into him, kissing me softly, holds me, we gaze into each other's eyes.

'This is it, I have to go, and I'll go down for this.'

'You're innocent, wait, Adam.' He leaves the tiny table and chairs and walks away from me, I watch him walk towards the cars which have just arrived at the party. Several police cars.

Mother, father and Mary stare with horror. The music goes off. Everybody has stopped dancing to watch Adam walking to the police, cuffed, head-guided into one of the cars, people looking on. Rebecca runs through the crowd, pushing past everyone, screaming, 'Adam, what the fuck is going on? It's my birthday, why are you arresting my brother?' She falls to her feet, slumps down, slamming her hands on the hardened ground punching like she wants to dig up the entire earth. Everybody has turned to speak to their friends, hands over mouths.

CHAPTER 22

✦✦✦✦

I'm in reception in Kensington police station, 2.10 am, being booked. I hand my watch, belt, shoes, laces and wallet over the counter, to the sound of drunks shouting from their cells. I state my name, fuming through gritted teeth and growling at the man checking me in.

Then I'm locked in a cell with a stinking unwashed silver basin, head in my hands, shaking my head about the embarrassment I've caused in front of everyone. Why tonight, why? It's obvious: this is a murder investigation and I am the number one suspect. Forefinger above my top lip; nothing but time on my hands now, no clock in the cell, just rusty pale white walls with stencils left by people writing on them, the graffiti of people being held in custody yet proud to leave their names all over the walls. How did they have the tools to do it?

With nothing to do, I just rest my head in my hands, refusing to lie down and close my eyes. I sit up and look at the CCTV camera above, growling under my breath. I look down at the dirty floor, fuming at the thought that I'll probably be in here until Monday at the earliest. DC Williams isn't on duty until Tuesday – I know his schedule, know that he will lead the interview. I'm a framed man. I may not even see daylight again if it's up to the bastard Jerry.

Two officers unlock the door, looking at them looking at me.

'How you are doing in here mate?'

'As good as it gets, what do you think?'

'Sorry about earlier, just doing our job, what about you? Did you?'

'Come on guys you know me, I wouldn't, she was my client.'

'Rumour has it you were having an affair with her.'

'You what?'

'just letting you know mate.'

'Come on, that's totally...'

'Adam, we know you, but your prints are on a glass in her place.'

'That doesn't mean I was fucking her!'

'This is off the record. Jerry showed Williams pictures of you two in your car.'

'And?'

'Had a PI on you both.'

'And that proves what exactly?'

'It doesn't look good mate.'

'None of this is good, he set me up.'

'You know the drill. You want a solicitor?'

'I didn't do it. Get Gary for me please, he will get me out tomorrow.'

'Hmm, doubt it, they got your sweater too, it will be Monday, you know how the system goes.'

'Where was it, where was my jumper? Because I can prove I walked into Nobu with it on and...'

'Can't go into it, sorry.'

'Come on guys, I need info. Don't bother with Gary, I'll wait to be interviewed alone, this is bullshit. Look, see, my sweater was taken from Nobu. What about their CCTV?'

'Nothing I'm afraid.'

'You got to be kidding me?'

'No.'

'This cannot be happening. The bastard!'

'Adam, if you got anything on him, anything at all, tell us.'

I sit back on the wall, sighing as loud as I can, drawing a huge breath, wiping the corners of my eyes with my fingers, pressing my hands over my face. I've got to tell them about the money laundering, got to get myself out of here.

'Nothing, I got nothing.'

'We know he's a shmuck, we know about his money

laundering. Do you know anything about that, anything at all?'

'Nothing guys, I got nothing.'

'Can't do a damned thing for you, mate.'

'What about a cup of coffee?'

'Yeah, I'll be back in a minute.'

They leave, locking the cell door. I lean over my knees with my head in my hands. This is it. If I open the laundering scandal, there is a way out of this. Still won't prove my innocence, they want to frame me for her murder, they've got my prints and sweater and I am totally fucked. I'll tell them he has gang connections as well as money laundering. But it has nothing to do with this inquiry, I have to prove somehow that it is all related.

I'm sweating in the humidity of the summer night, rocking back and forth on a concrete block with a dark, inch-thick, grey-stained mattress, biting the nail on my thumb.

The silver block opens on the grey door and a tray appears with a brown paper cup. I walk over to get it, sit back down sipping the hot coffee, burning my lips. My rights are being breached – no they're not. Confusion sets in, sitting upright all day, not seeing sunlight, refusing to eat. Not being able to take a walk outside. Fuck it. Pissing in the basin, stretching my back walking around the four walls, getting angrier as time goes on.

'You're not doing yourself any favours not eating.'

'What the fuck do you know? Fuck off.'

'Nice attitude you got there!'

'I said fuck off.'

I don't know the young change-over officer, he probably doesn't know me. I'm not allowed to read information under the confidentially act. I am totally fucked, never going to see daylight again. Treated like a real criminal, treated like the rest being put in cells; new arrivals screaming and throwing tantrums. Shit, I'll go straight to court, oh fuck, this is it. Collating my thoughts, knowing what is about to happen, knowing that it's highly likely I'll be remanded in custody, perhaps forever.

CHAPTER 23

✦✦✦✦

Text from Jerry: *You're late, where are you?*

Me: *Running late, been in the country at mother's for my birthday, be back lunchtime.*

Jerry: *Make sure you are.*

I dash inside and change into a cream knee-length skirt; white chemise, matching cream fitted jacket. I head out to the car and phone the court on Bluetooth surround. I take off my ring and place it in the overhead locker next to the mirror, pressing the black leather door shut. I hope they let him go. I look at the clock on the dash, 08.50. Traffic at a standstill. Phew, this is why I didn't want a car, fuck! I'm sitting in the heat, 21 degrees already. My hand is pressed to my forehead waiting for the cars in front to get a move on. I want to get to court so he can see me, see I was there for him. I wipe the tear away from my cheek, putting a strand of hair behind my ear.

Text to Jack: *Are you in work?*

Jack: *No.*

Me: *Why not?*

Jack: *In Marbella, work related.*

What the...?

I press the accelerator down, head to the courts, find a space, dial the parking meter number, enter my credit card details. Up the concrete steps, hand my handbag to the security guard, walk through a security screen in case I'm carrying a firearm. I hope he sees me in the courtroom.

Now I'm sitting outside Court 1, on a wooden bench, looking through my handbag for a mirror and lipstick. I look up to see solicitors and barristers walking past busily. Then I see the Irish bloke who came over to me asking me to have dinner with Adam two weeks ago.

'Hey, you, what are you doing here?'

'It's Adam, he is due in court.'

'You two finally got it together then?'

'Yeah, yes we did, thank you.'

'Ha, I didn't do a thing, I knew he wouldn't have the balls to ask you himself. You should have chosen me, you know.'

'Do you know why he's in court?'

'He works here.'

'I didn't catch your name last week, what is it?'

'Gary.'

'Oh gosh, he isn't here for work.'

'Are you hear to see him?'

'No, yes, he's in court, in that one there, he was arrested.'

'No way, what for?'

'Oh my god, I thought you two were like, best friends? Look, is there anything you can do to help him?'

'Sorry, but I sure will come into the courtroom with you, if you'd like? What has he done?'

'Nothing.'

'Then he wouldn't have been arrested then, would he? Wait here, I am going to find out some things.'

'You're so kind helping.'

'No worries love.'

'Okay.'

I look at Adam standing in a glass box in handcuffs, police either side of him, looking back at me and then straight ahead to the Judge. Gary walks in and sits down on the uncomfortable wooden benches.

'All rise. Mr Adam Freeman, please state your date of birth for the courts.'

'26th November 1973.'

'How do you plead?'

'Not guilty, your honour, it's an artifice your honour, I can prove it wasn't me, just give me a week or so?'

'How do you propose so, Mr Freeman?'

'Your honour, you know me, she was my client, I have collated evidence from my client, you'll see your honour.'

'You have been successful in your career. There is evidence that you were the last person to see her.'

'Your honour, I have evidence that Jerry Cunningham and Jack were at her residence after I left her alive and well, your honour.'

'Who is Jack? There is nobody in these statements mentioning Jack.'

'Your honour, I'm being framed. If you give me the time, I can provide you with all relevant evidence, that's why Jack's name isn't in the statements.'

'Bail is set. Mr Freeman, you have until Monday 9th September for your trial for the murder of Lucy Cunningham.'

Adam is uncuffed and transported down from the box. He walks over to us.

'Let's get out of here. Gary, what are you doing here?'

'Never mind that, what the fuck is going on?'

'He was set up by my boss.'

'Heard it on the news, thought Jerry did it, though they arrested him last time I heard the news.'

'I need to get to the bottom of this before I go down for something I didn't do. You going into work?'

'Not until lunch, I told him.'

'Come on.'

'Where to?'

'My house. Gary, you are coming too. I need to speak to you. Can you get to mine in twenty?'

'On my way.'

'Sophia, did you drive here?'

'Yes, parked there.' He takes my hand in his, walking quickly pulling me with him each step towards the car. He sits in the car, presses the button for the roof to unfold.

'You're not working for him, I forbid it.'

'This is a complete mess, what are you going to do, why can't I go to work?'

'It's too dangerous for you.'

'Jack is in Marbella Adam.'

'Who is Jack, how do you know him?'

'I got him promoted last Friday, he was supposed to start his new role today, and I texted him earlier and he said he is in Marbella. He was in the driver's seat that night in Jerry's car, I told you Saturday remember?'

'Got it.' Adam smiles at her.

'Got what?'

'Found a way to... never mind, that's why Jerry sent him to Marbella, it makes sense, see? Jack's gone, key witness, and Jerry is a cunning bastard.'

'I guess it does. I know what you're implying but if I don't show up for work...'

'Gosh I love you, smart woman. Yes it will look odd if you don't turn up, you do not go out to lunch with him, you say no to anything outside of work, you must not let on anything at all. Are you listening?'

'Yes, but I don't see what you're going to do?'

'Find Jack.'

'You know what he looks like?'

'No, do you have a picture?'

'No, but it's on his file in the office.'

'Right drop me here, I'll walk the rest, go into work, act like you normally do.'

'How is that?'

'I don't know, just like you I suspect.'

'Well everyone says I act like a bitch.'

'Act like that then.'

'What about your sister?'

'Bugger.'

'What?'

'I'll text her, find out if she's at work, if she is, she will kick off at Jerry.'

'I doubt that.'

'Why is that?'

'No one can get to him in his office. He hardly leaves it unless he comes to my office screaming at me in front of everybody. I just thought of something.'

'Go on?'

'Everyone's files are in Jerry's office.'

'And?'

'I have a key.'

'So, leave it for a couple of hours, then hold a meeting with him for something.'

'Like what? That won't work.'

'Why not?'

'It just won't.'

'Sophia, think of something.'

'I have.'

'Go on?'

'Remember that night in the Bell, your sister ran over to you both?'

'And?'

'Jack was at the bar ordering drinks, tall blonde, skinny, blue eyes, remember him? Adam, you really don't look well at all.'

'I'm thinking.'

'Think harder.'

'Sophia, you're not safe with me.'

'What does that mean?'

'Where's your ring?'

'Up there above the mirror, in that case.'

'Don't do anything rash. He had a PI on me, he knows you and I are dating. The process is probably still going on, he won't have just given up on getting pictures of Lucy and me. He has photographs of us two.'

'Seeing us in the car, oh my gosh, are they watching us now?'

'Perhaps.'

CHAPTER 24

✦✦✦✦

I open my Mac, stand up and put my lily on the windowsill, scratching my face. I slop back down, flump on my chair, and press the red answering machine to listen to thirty-seven messages from companies all wanting to go into next month's publishing. Sighing, I write notes in my Mac Book, leaving memos after each message to call back companies from A to Z. I remind myself to focus on work at hand, block everything out of my head, to knuckle down and do my job.

Caller ID buzzes on the black phone: Jerry calling.

'You're early, let me take you out for lunch, we need to discuss things.'

'Jerry, I have tons to do.'

'We're going out to lunch, I'm coming down for you. Get your cream jacket on.' How the fuck does he know what I'm wearing? No way am I getting out of this. Fuck!

'Where are we eating?'

'Ivy.'

Nice and public, sod it, I got questions as well.

'Fine, see you in a jiffy.'

I opt to leave my jacket on the seat, letting everyone know I am back, and it's way too hot to wear anyway. I wait with anticipation, swinging on my seat, legs crossed waiting for him to appear at the glass window, self-composed with a pen in my hand, tapping my teeth. Then I see him opening my door, peering around and smiling with his pathetic veneers.

'Grab your jacket then, come on.'

'It's way too hot out there, I'm fine like this.'

'As you like.'

As we walk towards the elevator everyone falls silent, looking down at their screens. Some are on the phone and look over at us both walking together, suspecting we are an item. A black car pulls up and the chauffeur gets out and opens a door. Paranoia strikes as I remember what Adam said earlier.

'You all right?'

'Fine, why?'

'Looks like you've seen a ghost.'

'Jerry, enough already, the Ivy is only up the road.'

'We're not going to the Ivy.'

'But you said...'

'I know what I said. Look, I just want to talk to you.

We're going to Nobu instead, less busy in there plus we get a private booth, no one ear wigging if you get me?'

'Huh, fine. How is Jack getting on in his new role?'

'Yeah, bright lad that kid.'

'Why isn't he at his desk?'

'Said he got man flu, really sounded full of it, if you ask me.'

'Oh, poor thing, why do they call it man flu? I haven't had a day off once until last week, it's just a cold, Jerry.' I'm trying to escape my real thoughts, to keep him thinking I am as stupid as I look. Trying my best to keep my composure together without him suspecting a thing. I know he probably realises I know the truth, but we're both entering the restaurant playing mind-games. I know it, he knows it too, but he is framing my fiancé and I'm going to get under his skin. Not sure how yet.

'Wine?'

'No thank you.'

'Why not?'

'I need a clear head for work and like I said, it's way too hot.'

'Chai then?'

'Yes please.'

'I'm having champagne.'

'Celebrating?'

'Yeah, yeah you could say that.'

'For what?'

'Seeing your cheating boyfriend go down for killing my wife.'

'Jerry, I had no idea, he cheated on me or you?'

'You didn't know? Here, look at these photographs.'

'I had no idea, I feel sick, that's....'

'Pull the other one, Sophia.'

'What do you mean?'

'You knew he was cheating on you.'

'I certainly did not.'

'I know you were with him outside court.'

'That didn't mean I knew he cheated on me.'

'Well he did kid, you and me both.'

'How do you know?'

'They were at it.'

'How do you know? They're just pictures, must say intimate ones at that, but there isn't any... do you have more, are there others of them, you know, making out sexually, or just these?'

'She had an affair with him, went on for over a year, that's why I kicked her out. She wanted a divorce. Yes, I have more in my apartment.'

'But you said on TV you were renewing your vows.'

'We were.'

'Then why? I don't understand.'

'Because of him, the prick, he wouldn't let her leave him.'

'Oh fuck, can you get me a glass, I need a drink?'

'No, you need a clear head.'

'Jerry I am not asking you, I'm telling you.'

'Knew it.'

'Knew what?'

'Knew you had it in you!'

'Knew I had what in me?'

'Fire.'

'Fire?'

'Yes, fucking fire inside of you. I knew you had balls from when you started as my intern. You were a cheeky cow then and you're a fiery bitch now. You are having a glass then?'

'Yes, I think I'm going to need the whole bottle.'

'Then you will. I got the funeral at 2.30.'

I almost spit my champagne out. My eyes are wide open, thanking heavens above he is looking at the menu, because I feel sick to my stomach. Adam seeing her for a bloody year and here I am having lunch with my boss for the first time ever and he's drinking, eating with me before his beloved wife's funeral. What the fuck is going on?

I scratch my scalp, blinking, trying to hold back the tears in my eyes. I'm almost choking on the bubbles, on the fact that he did have an affair for a year. Jerry had a PI on them. Now I am the dumb one. He asked me to marry him, in a moment of despair, worried about himself for committing murder, because I found out they were together. It all makes complete sense now. I'm furiously mulling over everything Jerry said, the truth, knowing that I knew he had a PI on them, knowing that the truth would hurt me, and here he is setting me free of my new cheating ex-fiancé.

CHAPTER 25

✦✦✦✦

With Jerry off to his lovely wife's funeral, I sit with elbows on my office desk, head in my hands, cupping my jaw with my palms and staring blankly at the Mac, not knowing what to think. I bite my lips together, nervously tapping my foot on the floor. I want to run out of the building, go home and curl up into a ball. I'm breathing in gasps and blowing out harder, trying to stop having an anxiety attack, making sure no one can see my face.

I stand up and shut the blinds. I hear my phone beeping in my bag and ignore it. I sit back down, wishing I could focus on work, but nothing. Just pick your bag up and leave, Jerry won't mind, he'll know why I left.

Phone keeps ringing. I let out a sigh and pick it up.

'Hello?'

Adam's voice. 'What on earth are you doing?'

'I'm at work.'

'I mean why did you have lunch with him? I specifically told you.'

'What I do is of no concern to you any more.'

'What does that mean?'

'it's clear enough.'

'No, no he has got into your head.'

'Bye Adam.'

'Listen to me please?'

'You have one minute.'

'I got a PI on him now, he is using you to get to me.'

'Oh really? I doubt that.'

'What does that mean?'

'He's been watching you and that poor woman for over a year.'

'Sophia that's rubbish, I have the pictures from Jerry's PI and they only show what you have seen, that morning last week in the car, that's all. Listen he would have more wouldn't he? Ask yourself that, why did you drink all the champagne in Nobu? See what he's doing? Why take you to lunch an hour before his wife's funeral? Think Sophia, pull yourself together, please?'

'How do you know how much I had to drink?'

'My PI took photographs of you both inside. He told me everything, even recorded you.'

'Recorded me?'

'Recorded him telling you lies. I have someone in Marbella now, I need the picture of Jack, Sophia, come on please don't let him do this to us.'

'I am really sick to my stomach of both of you. Leave me alone, Adam.'

I hang up the phone, not wanting to hear any more, then realise I know Jack said he was in Marbella, but Jerry told me he is sick with man flu. I reach for my handbag, grab my phone off the desk, take the elevator up to Jerry's floor. The door has been left ajar. I walk inside without turning the lights on, unlocking the cabinet and scour through the files in the cupboard, rummaging. I find Jack's cv file and photo. I ring Adam inside the elevator. Then I run out of the door back to the elevator, hit the ground floor button and run across the road into the Bell.

'Double vodka please.'

'Coming up.' I call Adam, pick up, quick, please? I lean on the bar, holding my head in my hands, stress making my shoulders tense.

A hand touches my shoulder.

'Hello Sophia.'

'Hello DC Williams.'

'Let me buy you another.'

'No thank you, I'm staying for this only, got to get back to the office but thank you.'

'Come on, let's have a bottle of wine together, I got the afternoon off.'

'I really should be getting back to my office, it's manic Monday I'm afraid.'

'Jerry and I play golf together, I've known him since

school, he's calling in soon. We all know Adam did it, got all the facts now. He isn't wired right, that ex of yours, cheating on you and his mrs on him.'

'Oh, really? In that case I'll stay and have a glass with you. Have you just been to the funeral? Is the wake in here?'

'Yes, no, it's around at the Castle. I just popped in here seeing you run in here, Jerry's driver just dropped me off. He's gone to get something from the office. He's calling in here and we're meeting everybody around the corner. What a waste of life, at that age, so beautiful, could have been you.'

'Huh yeah, I know, such a sad story, I can't get my head around it.'

Sitting there and knowing now what I didn't know then, these two framing my fiancé, I've got to do something. I reach out for a paper napkin and knock his wine glass over. He stands up before the whole lot can catch his trousers. I grab a napkin off the bar and hit redial. I leave the phone in my handbag, hoping it will go on answer phone.

'How did you say you knew Jerry again? Golf was it?'

'Yeah, old pals from school, we play every weekend, Lucy played too.'

'I would love to play golf, never tried it myself.'

'Then you must join, or I'll take you with me, we can pair up with another couple. Here he is, got you a glass Jezzer.'

'What you are you doing in here?'

'Having a wine with your friend.'

'Get back to work, come on the cars waiting.'

Jerry turns around scowling at me squinting his evil eyes holding onto the shoulder of DC Williams walking out towards the black chauffeur.

CHAPTER 26

✦✦✦✦

'What on earth was that about?'

'Adam, please tell me you heard that conversation, where is your PI?'

'No, I was coming to get you out of your office. My PI said he saw you run in here, said you were with Williams.'

'I rang you, did you pick up and hear the conversation?

'No, it was too loud. Would have gone to voicemail.'

'I have Jack's file here in my bag.'

'Jack's been sent off to Spain. Right let's go, you're not working for him any more, now do you trust me?'

'Yes, I need to go and get my things out of my office before he gets back.'

'I'm coming with you and, wait.'

'What?'

'I need to listen to that voicemail, wait.'

'Okay.'

'Nothing, it's all muffled. I waited around the corner watching you two at the bar, saw him put his hand on your shoulder, I saw the call, didn't want to interrupt.'

'We're on CCTV in here, proving that Jerry and Williams are friends.'

'Sophia, in a court of law it doesn't mean anything I'm afraid.'

'He invited me to play golf with him.'

'He did what? We're going to get your things out of that office.'

'Adam, this may or may not be relevant.'

'What?'

'You said earlier that he had a private thingy on us.'

'Investigator, yes. Why are you always drinking when you're in bother?'

'Well I wouldn't be bloody drinking if I wasn't going out or working with a...'

'Calm down, shh, what is it?'

'Today, Monday, Jack got promoted.'

'And?'

'Jerry paid me a huge salary, with a bonus, and then fired me.'

'Fired you just now?'

'No last Monday, see?'

'No, you're not making any sense.'

'Jerry promoted Jack, fired me, re-hired me, for what?'

'You got proof he fired you and re-hired you?'

'Yes.'

'And?'

'Why would he promote Jack, then send him off to Marbella, and tell me in Nobu that he's off sick with man-flu? Your private man has that in the recording?'

'Yes, let's go over and get your things out of that building.'

'We'll be on CCTV, he even knew what I had on earlier on the telephone.'

'He'll have it all over the place. He did it, my PIs are on it. We'll get him. I'll make sure we get to Jack first.'

We head across the street into the building, into the elevator, walk to my office, take my Mac off the table and jacket off the seat, leaving my lily plant on the windowsill. We walk back out of the office towards the elevator, hand in hand with Adam. The silver elevator door slides open and Jerry's inside, smirking at the two of us.

We take the stairs like fugitives on the run, my heart pounding in my chest, the humidity making my hair stick to my face and neck. We head out of the front concierge doors, walk towards separate cars parked next to the pub in the side street.

'Where are we going?'

'First yours, to pack. You're staying at mine, so I know you're safe. I'll follow you, let's go. Wait, you're over the limit. Get in here, I'll come and get your car later. Now do you see what a demonic idiot he is?'

'Yes.'

'What made you change your mind?'

'About?'

'About knowing who you were dealing with. What man takes his employee out for lunch an hour before he goes to his wife's funeral?'

'I know, the champagne got to my head.'

'You mean he got in your head.'

'A bit, yes. What would you have thought if the boot was on the other foot?'

'That's why I needed you out of his sight, after hearing the recording. I would have barged in the building to get you out of there.'

At home I pick up the suitcase I had from mother's, hurriedly throw more clothes inside, pass it to him and pack more clothes and shoes in the black Gucci suitcase, breathing heavily.

'What are we going to do, Adam?'

'Passport, have you got one?'

'Yes, don't know if it's in date though.'

'Where is it?'

'In the cupboard in the lounge, the one under the lamp. Are you allowed to leave the country?'

'You are.'

'Am I?'

'If your passport is in date, yes. I can't find it, where is it?'

'I'm packing, just keep looking. Where am I going?'

'Your brother lives in Australia, far enough?'

'I can't go there.'

'Why not?'

'Austin's in rehab, mum and dad are flying out to see him this week.'

'Perfect, you go with them.'

'I can't just go with them.'

'Why not?'

'They think I have a great career. Well, I did up to half an hour ago.'

'Sophia, you can stay with me. Timothy Briars lives on my street, they have machine guns, can't get safer than my house.'

'Then why pack me off to Australia?'

'Just a suggestion, if you didn't want to stay with me.'

'Why wouldn't I want to stay with you?'

'An hour ago you weren't sure about me, remember?'

'Adam, I'm certain about you. I told you it was the champagne and Jerry is so manipulative. Why do you think he got to where he got?'

'There are a lot of things you don't know about him.'

'Like what and who is Timothy Briars? That old PM?'

'Tell you later at mine during dinner, yes that old PM.'

'Are you cooking?'

'No.'

'Are we going out?'

'No.'

'Then how will we eat dinner?'

'Ever heard of ordering a take-away?'

'Funny.'

'What's even funnier is your passport is out of date.'

'Ha, really?'

'Just about to anyway, you have six months left. Have you been away recently?'

'Nope not since, phew, years ago, a family holiday in Cyprus. I'm ready, got everything for at least three to four weeks.'

'That's what we got, three to four weeks.'

'Until what?'

'My trial.'

'It won't come to that, not if you get to Jack first. You have your men on him, right?'

'Right.'

CHAPTER 27

✦✦✦✦

Adam is sitting opposite me on a white leather chair, eating like he's never been fed. I sip my wine and place the glass back on the table, making a clicking sound on the glass. My elbow is on the table, my hand resting on my cheek, looking over at him. He is sitting in complete and utter silence, not giving a glance in my direction.

I pick up the chopsticks, fiddling with the Japanese take-away. I'm hungry, but the food is full of additives and preservatives. I find some shrimp and delve into the vegetables and the plain flavour of the noodles. I'm eager to break the silence, talk about what we're going to do, what is he going to do, what Jerry's plans might be for us. Unimaginable – this is all turning into a nightmare. I'm just hoping Adam's men will find Jack and we can put Williams away with Jerry. I'm swallowing heavily with each morsel of food, trying my best to eat properly with the chopsticks.

I look over at him, cough quietly, hoping he will look up, say something to me, anything, but no, he carries on eating, sips his wine.

Eventually he looks at me.

'You're not hungry?'

'Hmm, doesn't really agree with me.'

'You have a great appetite. Eat up, you'll feel better, unless you don't like it?'

'Yes, I like it, just that...'

'What is it now?'

'I'm worried out of my mind, aren't you?'

'No.'

'Why not? This isn't something you can brush under the carpet, we need to discuss things.'

'Like what? It just isn't tenable.'

'So, we're just doing nothing?'

'That's right, nothing.'

'You have to be kidding me, what about…'

'I'm a suspect and on bail remember, I can't do anything. Let's just leave it to my men, they have it under control, they will collate the evidence. You need to print off the texts from Jerry and the bank statements showing all the money he has paid into your account. It will all work out.'

'Oh bugger.'

'What now?'

'What if he framed me too?'

'You mean with vast amounts of money? Did he give you a letter terminating your employment?'

'No.'

'Then how do you have proof?'

'Here, this text he sent me, that same day, look here?'

'So you banked almost half a million and you had no termination of contract of employment, just this stupid text?'

'Yes.'

'We're fucked.'

'Why are we? We can still find Jack, prove he is lying.'

'You don't get it, do you?'

'No, I don't see what you're getting at, actually.'

'Clever bastard.'

'Excuse me?'

'Jerry, the bastard!'

'I really don't get it, why are you shouting at me?'

'Darling I'm sorry, been locked away for a day and a half, trying to figure things out, excuse me. I mean, somewhere Jerry has fucked up, he is backtracking, he is up to something and I just don't know what. I know he has property in Marbella.'

'Think, darling.'

'How? like a criminal?'

'If that what it takes, then yes.'

'Did you have access to his business accounts?'

'No, he uses Elaine the accountant, works on Sage accounting.'

'You friends with her?'

'Yes, I filled in the weekly spreadsheet of all employees, who worked what hours, and sent it to her weekly. She pays everybody monthly; she has access to his business account.'

'How did he pay you?'

'In a payee bank slip, as per just a year's salary and a bonus upfront.'

'Phew, that's a weight off then. My phone, where is it, I can hear it, where is it?'

'Over there, in the lounge.'

I hear muffled sounds he walks away down the hall. I clear the table, put the dishes in the dishwasher, throw the empty plastic take-away in the recycling bin, wipe the glass table. Then I walk into the lounge and sit with my feet upon the pouf, resting my head back, sighing with a small sense of relief, but knowing we have a long way to go. I'm housebound, scared what the outcome will be...

Phone starts beeping in my bag.

'Hello mum.'

'Did he do it?'

'Don't be so ridiculous!'

'Why are you insisting on this engagement?'

'Mother listen, I quit my job, I am living at Adam's.'

'You did what?'

'It's my boss mum, he did it, and he's trying to frame Adam and me.'

'You? Your father wants you, one second love.'

'Get away from him, come home right away, you hear me love?'

'Dad, ugh, he didn't do it, it's my boss, we're sorting this.'

'Do you want that lawyer?'

'Dad I have to go, I'll call you soon.'

'We're going to see Austin, come with us, get away from him for three weeks.'

'Dad, I am fine here, I need to stay here. Bring Austin home with you guys.'

'The number for the lawyer is being sent to your email, ring him.'

'I'm not in trouble.'

'No but he is, he'll sort it for him, if he is innocent like you said. It's your boss, I knew it!'

'Bye, give Austin a kiss from me.'

'Parents?' says Adam.

'Huh, yeah.'

I scratch my head, my curls over my face, sitting forward with my elbows resting on my thighs, head in my hands. I listen to him on the phone, watch him pace up and down.

'Who was that?'

'Mick and Terence, my men. They're on a yacht opposite Jack.'

'Really, where?

'Puerto Banus, on a yacht owned by Jerry.'

'Oh goodie.'

'They're watching him from a yacht next to his. I'm renting it.'

'You're renting a yacht next to Jerry's?'

'Yes. What about if I fly out there?'

'You can't leave the country.'

'Yes, but we can take the jet, I'll make sure no one tails us. We can do this together.'

'What if Jerry has people watching Jack too?'

'Oh, he will, I am certain of that. You need to see Jack, he trusts you.'

'How am I to get him alone with you? He doesn't know you, he might get intimidated.'

'You got any other ideas? I'll sort arrangements out, make sure you two are alone, with my men watching.'

'What about Jerry's men? Oh, I'm really not sure about this.'

'Jack trusts you?'

'Yes, kind of, but he must know why he was packed off to Marbella.'

'Don't be so sure about that.'

'Why not?'

'Jerry would have told him a new job, a new promotional something. Jack won't have a clue what's going on.'

'How can you be so certain? What if Jerry paid him to... you know, strangle her?'

'Doubt it. But we can't rule anything out I suppose.'

'Then what if this trip is a waste of time, what if you get in trouble too?'

CHAPTER 28

✦✦✦✦

There's a private limousine waiting on the tarmac by the steps to the jet. Heat and wind blow humidity into my face; I wipe my hair back and step down onto the ground in my black knee-length dress, carrying my brown Louis Vuitton hand luggage. I forgot that black absorbs heat. I walk to the car and the chauffeur opens my door.

Adam gets into the front seat, passing the driver something. As we drive to immigration at the gates, the chauffeur passes something and our passports to a man in a white box, big black eyes, Roman nose, pierced small lips. The man bends down to look at us both, nods and sets the barrier free, and the car heads out of Malaga airport towards Marbella, along the road that back in the 1990s was called the 'road of death'. I'm taking in the beauty of the buildings, the countryside and all the picturesque scenes. Where are we staying, will we be caught, will Jerry have a tail on us? Air conditioning on, I'm sitting in the back completely and irrevocably in love with my fiancé, but I'm questioning inside who he is, knowing he paid the immigration officer to get him into the country, knowing he is rich, knowing he has millions if not billions, but I don't care about the money he was left by his father, from all he told me last night.

I'm still in a trance from last night, feeling confused as options run through my head. We sit up in bed for hours talking about his brilliant father. *Who is my fiancé? Could he be a criminal after all? Am I in danger? Should I have gone with mum and dad and let him tie up these loose ends?*

Adam's father owned a handful of mansions in London and Surrey, some in the UK and several in Spain and Portugal, then sold them all seven years before his sudden death from a heart attack. Ten years earlier, after getting Paul McCann, a notorious heavy in London, off on three counts of murder, the press had been all over him and McCann. Adam's great-grandfather had owned several farms in Cirencester, Tetbury and Surrey. The properties accumulated and passed onto his grandfather, who sold some of the farms and bought properties in the south in the 1930s and 70s, passing them onto Adam's father. But he had no interest in the properties; all he cared about was being the best barrister he could be. Even though the criminals paid him buckets of illicit cash, his dad's fate caught up with him in the end.

As far as I know Adam owns only his place on Cabell Street, a few doors down from that old MP Briars. Adam just gave me his entire family history and I listened as I lay on his chest, closing my eyes, nodding and making sounds to assure him I was listening.

I'm resting my right elbow on the car door, flickering over my confused thoughts from last night, my right hand on my forehead looking out of the window, wondering just who is sitting in the front seat. I bite my lower lip. Is he a big-time criminal? Sounded like his father was happy defending horrid criminals. Maybe he got in way over his head; perhaps he had no other option. Knowing my fiancé is proud of his job, I'm not happy with all this mess, not one bit. What if he is playing with fire, what if Jerry kills him, kills us all?

We're climbing up a mountain in the limousine, in a low gear, up a dusty pathway, it's not even a road. Red and brown soil, stones and pebbles rubbing on the tyres as we drive upwards towards a huge pink villa. I look down through the back windscreen and see the Mediterranean behind. There are villas down the hillsides on either side but nothing close to us. In front a triple white garage door starts unwinding, and I see three cars parked inside.

'We're here, I'll get your bag.'

'Okay.'

'José, park next to the Lamborghini, then come inside, you're staying with us.'

'Yes sir.'

'Come on in, I'll show you around, hope you like it.'

I follow him up seven tiny white polished marble steps and in through double tinted glass doors with crystal handles. Adam presses the keypad inside the cool air hallway and silver electric doors slide open either side. He takes my hand and we enter the white-open plan lounge area with terracotta plant pots and tall areca palm trees spaciously set out opposite one another. Adam leads me to the right, presses a button, and the white blinds unwind, revealing windows overlooking the Mediterranean. He takes my hand, we step over white marble flooring and onto the next room, blinds unwinding. We're looking out onto a decking area. He opens the doors and leads me outside, we walk past a huge silver barbecue. Soft white seats with matching round pillows and a ten-seater seating area. Around the corner, a large pool, like a mirage above the mountain, and the view of the Mediterranean, all you can see.

'Like it?

'I love it.'

'It's yours.'

'Pardon?'

'It's ours.'

'Then I definitely love it.'

'Come on I'll show you our new home.'

'You mean you haven't lived here before?'

'No, bought it the same night you said yes.'

'Whose are the cars?'

'Mine, bought those too, got them sent here.'

'Really?'

'Yes, I have lots of options, now you've said yes. See, before you, I really had no idea what I wanted from my life. You made me.'

'I did?'

'Had the cleaning company come around this morning, whilst you were in the shower. It cost me 1200 euros at such late notice. Do you like it?'

'I love it. Ha ha, show me around.'

'Okay, I'm not sure, only seen pictures. I got the codes and everything in the email, through my solicitor. Come on, let's look around our new home.'

'We're living here?'

'Whenever we want to come home to Spain, yes.'

'Wow, you're really full of surprises. Come on then.'

'Look, the kitchen is underground, out of the heat, come on.'

We walk through a white door and down three white carpeted steps into the biggest white and silver vinyl kitchen. Three crystal chandeliers sparkle above. The cleaners had left six silver vases of white lilies jotted around the outskirts on separate mantelpieces, vases glowing off the lights above. There's a huge light blue tinted glass dining table in the centre with ten soft white tall cushioned chairs, and a brand-new smell. We walk around some kitchen cupboards with no handles – they open with electric sensors when I raise my palms. I walk backwards and the doors stay open, walk nearer and put my hands together either side of the vinyl and they close. Another three doors without handles. The fridge-freezer opens on the left. I walk backwards and the doors close straight away.

At the back of the kitchen, a door opens, and we go up another set of three marble stairs, Adam and the driver in tow, to the other side of the house. There's a huge white and silver washroom on our right, crystal door handle. We all look inside, it's big enough for six people. On the left is a large turquoise room, white blinds on the window.

The window overlooks the mountain. We walk through another door into a bedroom with a queen-sized bed, neatly made. Adam presses the button for the blinds; this window looks out over the mountain. Leaving the room, we walk down a white darkened hall and spotlights on the floor light up. Then it's up two flights of wooden stairs with white carpet in the centre, and spotlights on the ceilings automatically come on as we approach. Two bedrooms opposite each other, one facing the mountain, the other the Seaview.

'You go down, bring our bags inside,' says Adam to José. 'Yours is the bedroom downstairs, make yourself at home.'

'Yes sir.'

In the hallway, there's a huge centre marble block with a silver vase of lilies. Opposite the window, a door leads into another bathroom. I bite my lip, nodding: 'Guest's bathroom, right?'

'Right.'

'And down the hall?'

'I'll follow you, go on.' I turning the crystal handles around, try to pull open the double doors, but I can't get in.

'The code's on my phone downstairs, but we can get up here through the other side of the building too.'

'We can?'

'You mentioned a lift in London.'

'Adam, that was because of all the stairs, come on.'

We run back through the hallway and down the stairs like a pair of kids in a sweetshop. Going down back into the kitchen, he pulls my arm. 'This way.' As we pass the turquoise room, I realise I hadn't seen the rest of the inside. There's a stone statue of a naked man seven feet tall and an opposite matching statue of a naked woman. Wow. We come to a room on the left, a massive white lounge. He presses the silver button and the blinds unfold. A large TV is on one wall and there is a fluffy 12-seater white sofa, a blue tinted glass table in the centre and a chandelier above. Outside the same view as the turquoise room; the only difference is a huge olive tree looking down from the window and another on the right.

I can almost touch the leaves.

Closing the blinds, shutting the door, we're back into the two main lounges. I'm feeling overwhelmed.

'There are two doors to the elevator.'

'Two?'

'Yes, one here, look.'

He takes my hand, leads me to a dining area set inside, another petite white vinyl kitchen. The double doors open to a third private terrace with a small white table with two chairs.

'Press it then.'

'Press... oh the button?'

'Yes.'

'There isn't one.'

'Oh, the codes. One minute, where is my phone?'

'No clue.'

'Wait, it's down in the kitchen.'

'Hurry up.'

'One sec darling.'

'Hurry up Adam.'

'What's the rush?'

'I need a pee.'

'Got it, press 5678.'

'It's not working.'

'Wait, that's the front door system, try 7856.'

'OK, it's working.'

I kiss him softly and press my legs together, wishing the doors would open. A little beep sounds and the doors open. He's kissing me in the elevator and I'm so excited I'm almost peeing myself. The doors open and there's a colossal room with a mahogany queen bed, white pressed linen. At the other end of the room is a huge white free-standing bathtub, standing on silver legs.

'Oh my gosh I love it, it's half the size of the house.'

'Nice eh?'

'Adam where... do we have a real bathroom?'

'Look up there.'

'Oh my gosh.'

I dash past the bed, then back, and see the stairs opposite running up to the washroom with terracotta brick flooring, blue stained-glass panels, our private bathroom overlooking the bedroom and pool area. I look around, taking in the beauty. There's a shower on my right, no bath tub, a set of terracotta bricks filled with fluffy white towels, two massive sinks side by side, mirrors on the glass panels, lights that will go as low or high as you want, two toilets and an inset bricked set of six cupboards to fit everything in. It's big enough for high tall vases filled with flowers. I see him on the bed, watching me, smiles up in my direction.

'Well?

'Are you kidding me?' I run down the stairs, jump on the bed and lean over him on the bed, and we roll around kissing and giggling into one another's eyes.

'Hold on you, slow down, we have things to do, I have to go somewhere.'

'Can't we just stay here for now?'

'We have nothing in, come on, let's go downstairs, you're going shopping.'

He takes my hand down the hallway and I breathe in the scent and the beauty of our summer home.

'Take her to the supermarket, José. You're going shopping, here's my card. I want you to fill this place up with food and drink.'

'I have my own card, you shouldn't use yours Adam. And I'll use mine.'

'As you wish, take her, fill the car up, buy everything.'

'Where are you…?'

'Out, don't worry, just meeting a few clients. I'll be back before six, shall we have a barbecue later?'

'Yes okay, Adam. Can you please ask him to wait in the car? I need to change, I'm going to fry in this dress.'

'Okay, see you later.'

CHAPTER 29

✦✦✦✦

Adam is dressed in white linen trousers, a black T-shirt, gold Ray Bans, black sandals. He drives through Marbella to the MGM Boxing Club and pulls into a space behind a silver Bentley. The sun pierces the branches of the palm trees as he opens the boot and takes out a black gym bag. He slams the boot lid down and walks over to the black tinted windows of the club. A familiar blonde smiles at him from behind the counter and hands him a black tag. She's wearing a knee-length red dress, two thin straps over the shoulders, a pearl necklace and matching earrings enhancing her natural olive skin. Dark blonde straight hair, red and black Louis Vuittons.

'Welcome back Adam, so nice to see you again,' she says in Hispanic accented English. Her big brown eyes glisten and a beguiling smile shows perfect veneers and full ruby lips.

'Yeah, you too. Is he in?'

'Yes, he never leaves the office since his brother got shot. Lives and breathes here since then.' She nods to the office.

'Thanks Maria.'

'You're welcome.'

He presses the black tag on the glass panel doors and they open automatically. He walks past six sets of boxing rings; first the amateurs, no older than fifteen, red and black headsets, red gloves, feet stepping back to front, side to side, sweat dripping down their arms, chests and legs. Then the lightweight fighters preparing for their first matches, then the heavyweight professionals punching the daylight out of each other. The coach whistles, but that doesn't stop them. One last blow is thrown, and Kim Wright is knocked out.

Adam enters the dressing room, quickly fitting a circular silver device onto the back of the collar of the tailor-made suit of Matt King. He gets changed, puts clothes on the rail, gym bag into locker 13, and heads out to the gym. He does fifty press-ups before the fifteen-minute weights, then throws a black towel around his neck and heads to the showers, glancing over at Jamie the coach in the changing room patting down Wright's eye, putting Vaseline over the wound. Junior is talking to Matt wiping off his sweat: 'I did it Dad, I did it.'

'Jerry's got your back,' Matt King mutters under his breath through gritted teeth.

'You have to knock him out in the fourth. You got him, you did it, but you took too long. You got to do it better than this son, you hear me?'

Wright gets off the table and walks over to the junior King. 'Never going to happen mate, never. I'll get you on Saturday, you're done.'

'Ha, look at you, you're done mate, you'll never take me down.'

Showered and dressed, Adam walked towards the office, watching them all still practising. He knocks on the door and a buzzer and green light give the go ahead. He walks in and takes a seat, stared at Kenny's darkened grey gaze, watching him sip his bourbon.

'Let me get you a glass, here, help yourself,' Kenny says in his Irish accent, smirking. 'You've been here, what, an hour, and you show up here? What you been up to?'

'You have to get out of this, you listening? How much have you had?'

'Not enough.'

'Ken, you fucking stink man, you have to climb out of this. What the fuck are you in here hiding for? Get showered and come out with me, we'll drive out of town, you need to get out for fuck's sake.'

'No, they want me too.'

'They can get you in here, it's not the perfect hiding place is it?'

'You know what, you're right, glad you showed up. Maria thinks I'm going crazy, she keeps badgering me to leave here but it's the only secure place. Fuck it, let's get out, come on.'

'I'm not taking you out like that. Get a shower, put on some fresh clothes, you nutter.'

'Give me ten, I'll meet you at your car.'

Sitting in the car with the air con on, Adams listens through the tiny earpiece to Matt's monologue, water in the background so he struggles to hear. He watches as Maria opens the door to a delivery man who hands her a big bouquet of white lilies. He smiles to himself; she's got an admirer.

Kenny is in the shower lathering soap over his body, washing his grey, thinning hair, looking at himself in the tinted mirrors. He rinses off and dries himself, puts on a pink Ralph Lauren polo shirt and navy denims and sprays himself with Roja Parfums Imperial. He looks through his collection of sunglasses and chooses a pair, then grabs his Gucci wallet and heads to reception. 'Anybody calls I'm in the office in a meeting. Phew, look at you, you look good.' He sees the flowers,

'Who they off?'

'I don't know, there's no card.'

'You finally dating then?'

'Maybe, maybe not.'

'Ha, I'm out for the rest of the day, go for it.'

'Where are you going?'

'Out.'

'Yes, at last!' It's looking good. Maria arranges the flowers in a vase on the counter. Ken turns at the door to look back at her, then Matt walks past and pats her bottom.

'Drive Adam, get us out of here.'

'What do you know about Matt, and why is he putting his son in the ring with Wright?'

'It's complicated.'

'Well?'

'Look, they're paying me a fortune.'

'He's going to kill him.'

'That's the way it is, you know how my fights go. Where are we going anyway?'

'The harbour.'

'No, too risky.'

'Have you heard the news? I'm being framed.'

'You?'

'Yes, me.'

'What for?'

'It's complicated.'

'Well, we got something in common after all. Let's get out of town, how about the Terrace?'

'Ok, but only one, I've got business to attend to and I need your help.'

'What kind of help?'

'Bugging the changing rooms.'

'All of them?'

'Yeah.'

'Why, what information do you need? I got it all.'

'Kenny, I don't think you have. The fight this Saturday night, it's down to Jerry, right?'

'Yeah, he's orchestrating the whole thing, the slimy retard, thinks he owns Marbella. I'm the one who owns Marbella.'

'That's my point, he framed me for murdering his wife.'

'Oh! You didn't kill her, did you?'

'Me? Are you fucking kidding me?'

'I heard about it, but you, why you?'

'She hired me, he got photos, you know the rest. You ever had an amateur fighter in, British, twenties, blonde, lightweight, goes under the name of...'

'Jack.' They both say it at the same time, just as they pull into a space close to the Terrace pub.

'He's being trained by Matt too.'

'I should have said this earlier Kenny, I'm sorry about your brother.'

'Thanks. Danny didn't take it too well, he's gone on holiday to Majorca with his Mrs and my baby niece. He won't come here any more, don't want nothing to do with the club either. I feel like some fucker's going to shoot me too.'

'Paranoia will kill you before anyone shoots you, plus you own Marbella, you've got all the bars and restaurants.

Jerry's just trying to fuck with you, paying you for a rigged fight for his own gratification, the bastard.'

'Let's just go and sit at that table, soak in some vitamin D, drink a beer.'

'Sounds good to me. You look kind of pale, you need it.'

'You flirting with me?'

I'm sitting watching Kenny relax, arms stretched, neck rolling backwards, leaning forward to take a drink from his iced glass of beer, smiling to himself. The terraced area is filling up, all eyes on Kenny; even the waitresses flirt around him, all dreaming they could be Mrs Kenny O'Connor, not realising he's gay. Nobody knows because he flirts with all the ladies, buying them champagne, slapping their arses as they walk past. He keeps his sex life a secret.

A tall man rolls his yellow Harley into a space, and all eyes turn at the sound of the exhaust. Body tanned, skull tattoos, women's faces on his arms, big blue eyes, short brown hair. He smiles over at Kenny, who's sipping his beer, paying no attention, playing hard to get. I watch the scenario, the women watching this handsome freak show, the exhaust still revving for Ken's attention.

CHAPTER 30

✦✦✦✦

I'm walking around Carrefour with José in tow, both pushing shopping carts filled with sparkling arrays of waters, oils, wine vinegar, toiletries, household goods, wines, beers, fresh fruits, nuts, vegetables, a selection of meats from the deli department, copious amounts of everything, uncertain how long we are staying. We stroll around the aisles looking at the shelves, jars of sundried tomato, honey, olives, vine leaves, sage, oregano, parsley, thyme, spinach, mint, dill, chives, coriander, lengthy salt and pepper shakers in pinewood, a selection of cheeses. I come to a halt, scratching my head thinking I am missing something. Yes – soil, plant pots for the herbs to grow on the patio.

'Where are they?'

'Where are what, ma'am?'

'José, you can call me Sophia. The erm, how do you say in Spanish, *maceta tiesco*?'

'Plant pot?'

'Si.'

'Over there. How many will you need?'

'Ten?'

'We should pay, fill the car up and come back. You want soil also?'

'Si, gracias, okay, let's check out.'

We pile everything into the back of the car, fill it to the brim with bags, too much. We smile at each other, get into the front and press the air con.

'We can come back to get the pots.'

'José, you're too kind, gracias. Ooh, can you just stop at that shop, see on the corner?'

'More shopping?'

'No, just a quick look, I won't be long.'

I open the door of Bella Donna and walk into the quiet air-conditioned shop. Strolling around I picked up a long white linen skirt, matching chemise, a big round woven hat, flat blue and white shoes, a white knee-length skirt and matching jacket, a pair of grey linen trousers.

'May I help you?' A petite blonde, short hair, tired sun-kissed skin, wrinkles around her lips, takes the clothes from my arms. 'You like me to gift wrap?'

'No, gracias, I'll keep looking.'

'I'll fold these for you.'

'Thank you.'

A wavy ankle-length grey skirt with white buttons on the front, a pair of light brown flat shoes. I hold up a red dress with shoulder straps, a pair of blue Ray Bans in my free hand, and study a pair of white Louis Vuittons, checking the size.

'You would like to try?'

'I'll take all these but yes, I'll try on this dress with the shoes.'

'I'm sure they will look just perfect on your figure. Let me see when you are ready.'

Conscious of the time I am taking, I enter the crushed brown velvet room, sit on the chair and look into the mirror, cheeks blushing from the excitement of all my pretty clothes, the new house, new life, getting married. I try on the dress and shoes and like what I see.

As I open the curtain, I catch sight of a woman wearing a red dress slipping into another changing room.

'What do you think?'

'Mamma mia, you look perfect, I knew you would.'

'I'll wear them now, can you take off the tags please?'

'Of course, would you like the box for the shoes?'

'Yes please... oh no, keep the box, my car is full and the driver is waiting.'

'The total is seventeen thousand euro please.'

'Oh gosh, my purse is in the car over there.'

'No problem, I wait.'

'Thank you, I'll be back in a minute.'

As I cross the busy road a car speeds past, almost

knocking me down. Idiot! I bite my lip and remember to look left and right on the way back. I hand the lady my card and pick up several bags, the goodies wrapped in beige tissue paper. I take the receipt and put the card back into my Chanel purse.

'Thank you so much.'

'Watch the road.'

'You saw that?'

'Yes, take care. Come back soon, it was a pleasure to meet you, can I put you on my mailing list?'

'Maybe next time, thank you again.'

José is watching as I hobble across the cobbled road, his hand over his mouth, perhaps wondering where all those bags are going to go.

'Here, ready.' I squeeze the bags on the floor by my feet, some on my knee, barely able to see ahead.

'You sure we can go back to the house now, are you really finished Mrs Sophia?'

'Yes José, sorry you had to wait so long, I just...'

'I know, women and shopping.'

Looking out of the window I see the woman in the red dress, identical to the one I was wearing, walk out of the shop empty handed. Hair in a perfect straight bob, same shoes, just red and black. I hope José didn't notice. I have to get out of this dress when I get home.

'What colour pots would you like?'

'It's okay, we can go another day.'

'What colour?'

'Did you see the shiny blue ones?'

'Yes, I think they will look good on the patio, are you growing the herbs?'

'Exactly.'

'Tomatoes too?'

'Oh, a good idea, I would like to, as the house is sustainable, I might grow potatoes too. How much longer, José?'

'About twenty minutes.'

Taking in the road signs, familiarising myself with the shops, bars and restaurants, I recognise the road ahead. As we turn right I see Adam driving down and turning in the opposite direction to us.

CHAPTER 31

✦✦✦✦

I hear two other bikes in the distance out of sight; a six-foot-three tattooed muscle man switches off his engine, gets off his Harley and walks towards the table opposite. Two bike engines getting closer, what the fuck is this, a Harley bike show? The bikes get closer, and I see men in black balaclavas pointing their guns at us and hear gunshots. I shout 'get down!', then grab his arm and pull him off his chair. One shot hits his arm, one skims my shoulder, there's blood everywhere splattering over me. I look down at Kenny's arms over his head. Everyone's screaming and running in circles trying to flee and there wasn't a thing I could do. The tattooed guy has fled, no one around. I can still hear the sound in my head, like thunder.

'You okay?' I say to Kenny.

'My fucking arm! You see them, told you Adam, didn't I?'

'Come on, we're leaving.' I look around to see if the bastards are still in sight and grab Kenny's good arm. 'Get in.'

'Fucking told you, where are we going?'

'Got to take you to the hospital.'

'You are fucking kidding me! Drop me off at my gym.'

He's screaming as I drive off as fast as I can, 'fuck, fuck, fuck, fuck!' I slow down and head for the harbour pressing the sound device on in my ear through the wi-fi. Nothing I can hear; maybe out of range. I look down on my arm and blood is pouring softly downwards, droplets on the leather. Kenny's holding onto his arm and it's pouring with blood.

'I'll come back for you. Where is Maria?'

'Gone, the gyms closed for two hours, siesta shit.'

'See you in an hour.'

I've got to go to the fucking house and change, fuck, I hope she's still shopping. I drive up towards the house, thinking come on, don't be in, please don't be in. I smear the blood off my phone, trying to see the code to get inside. Fuck sake Kenny! Or was it a hit on me? I'm showering and banging my fist on the brick, thinking the only thing to do is find the source, drive to the harbour, get a coffee and be in earshot. I'll call the lads on the yacht and find out who those bullets were meant for. I dress in my blue polo shorts and another black T-shirt.

I pat my wound with a paper towel on my shoulder, but nothing's working – alcohol? Where is there some? Come on, come on, think!

I open my black bag and take out a bottle of Yves Saint Laurent La Nuit l'Homme and spray my shoulder, pulling more paper off the bathroom rail and pressing down, my face gurning, pressing my lips together. I put another black T-shirt over the first.

The phone starts beeping in my linens on the floor.

'Yes?'

'Jerry's Azteca is leaving the port.'

'Where is Jack?'

'Not with him.'

'Why not?'

'Went for a bike ride.'

'What you got, anything?'

'Just about the fight. Everyone is placing their bets, I heard Jerry laughing.'

'Who's on board?'

'Someone named Matt King, but you know him.'

'I'll be down in twenty, you know where.'

I change cars and drive down tapping my finger on the steering wheel, keeping the cabriolet up behind the black Porsche. I turn right and in the corner of my eye I see the driver pulling up towards the house. I dial Sophia.

'Hey you, you've been a while, what did you buy?'

'Hey yourself. Just about everything we need for the house. Oh, I went clothes shopping too. Was that you?

Why have you changed cars and why not put the roof down? It's bloody hot.'

'Which shall I answer first? Can you prepare some salads and drinks? We're having some guests later.'

'Okay, what time?'

'Later.'

'Adam, is everything okay?'

'Perfect.'

'It's going to take me ages putting all of this into three kitchens.'

'Three?'

'Yes, the one in the barbecue area too.'

'Ah, about that.'

'What?'

'The barbecue is off.'

'Off, why?'

'Just light stuff, salads, you know nibble foods and drinks in ice buckets.'

'Whoa, Adam it's going to take me ages, prepping salads and nibbles.'

'Okay, ice buckets with wine and champagne too.'

'We haven't got any Adam.'

'Send José.'

'Okay, see you later, bye.'

I look at José, and my mouth opens in a circle. His eyes are wide.

'José, would you be so kind and help me?'

'Sure, what would you like?'

'Could you drive back and pick up like erm, ten bags of ice, ten silver champagne buckets, and a case of the best wines and champagne please? Here is my card.'

'That's not necessary, I pay, your husband pays me.'

CHAPTER 32

✦✦✦✦

Five trips up and down in the elevator and at last I'm kicking off my shoes. The cool marble floor feels wonderful as I dash around the first petite kitchen with bottled water, two cases of white wine and another two of rosé, stacking them into the glass wine fridge. I look for a bowl for the fruit, but no, it means another run out. I'm sure there will be other things I forgot to buy.

I put some of the meat in the barbecue fridge and go downstairs to collect the rest of the bags and fill the main kitchen as quickly as possible, placing the herbal plants on the outside patio. I collect all the empty bags and realise we have nothing to put the rubbish in, *shit, shit!* I don't know José's number and I don't know my way around. Hmm... sat nav!

Keys, I don't know where he keeps them, they won't

be in the garage and he did say later, but that could mean an hour…

I dial Adam, trying to catch my breath. 'Hey, huh, I only bought foods and… I need lots of other stuff and I don't have José's number, I sent him out for champagne and…'

'Soph, calm down, breathe. Take the Mercedes, type the name of the supermarket into the sat nav, it's not that difficult.'

'And the keys?'

'There aren't any.'

'What?'

'Open the kitchen drawer by the door, there's a white label attached to a black circle. You just have to press the centre, so panic over.'

'Great, ok, see you later.'

'You shall indeed.'

Emptying the bags of clothes on to the floor I find the blue flat shoes and slip them on, then grab my bag, enter the elevator code and head for the car. I press the centre as instructed and a sound comes from the car and the lights flash. Opening the door, I look at all the buttons, searching for the ignition – nothing. *Shit, what the heck! How do I start it, where is…* I press the radio switch, look for the navigator. I type in 'Carrefour' and squeeze the black circle in my right hand – whoa, the engine's started! *How the fuck?*

I look down at the small electric device in my hand,

then press it again and the engine stops. I press again and it starts again. Ok, I have that worked out, now where is the handbrake? I scour the buttons, pressing one at a time, scared I may drive straight into the wall if I hit the accelerator by accident. I keep my foot on the brake, slowly revving the engine, and wipe my face with both hands. I look back at the steering wheel, look at the TV and see a button with R on it. Press it... *hey ho*, I slowly reverse, *yes and thank you Jesus*. I press D and drive slowly across the crunching gravel. I start following the instructions from the sat nav. I smile and silently congratulate myself.

It is so hot in the car that sweat is dripping down my face. I wonder where the air con is, but I am concentrating on the sat nav and don't want to pull over, so I open the windows, laughing at myself.

At the supermarket I drive around the car park, nervously wondering how to stop. Is there an S button for stopping? I look for a large space to pull into, slowly enter it and press the disc.

In the store, moving as quickly as possible, I buy an assortment of glass bowls, cutlery, a beautiful dinner set – make that two – plastic food containers, freezer bags, linen napkins, paper towels, plus many more necessary items I had forgotten, the last of which was baguettes. Close to the bread counter I noticed an orange juice maker described as a 'por favor naranja machine.' I indicate that

I would like it and the assistant looks into my shopping cart, both of us knowing it won't fit.

'Uno momento por favor, you pay, we bring to car, si?'

'Si, por favor.' I dash over to buy a large bag of oranges and make my way to the tills.

Back at the car I pack it carefully, the heavy boxes in the boot with the lighter bags on top, the big bag of oranges on the back seat. A man approaches carrying the boxed-up orange machine. He smiles and places the box next to the oranges.

I call Adam, but he answers abruptly, saying, 'I am in the middle of a meeting.'

'Sorry, I'm not sure of the way back home.'

'Where are you?'

'Carrefour.'

'The sat nav knows your starting point, type that in.'

'Really? Okay, thanks, bye.'

The phone clicks off. After all the hype, I suddenly feel alone, and insecurity creeps in. He's left me, no, he's left me with José, right there and then. Fuck his salad and nibbles.

Reaching the house, I pull into the garage, take out the oranges and walk to the elevator.

There are blood spots on the ground.

'José, are you okay?' I walk outside, shouting up to see if he's outside upstairs. I go up in the elevator.

'José, are you OK?'

'Si, I am here, look, I got your pots.'

'You planted them, wow, thank you José. Are you hurt?'

'No, I am not hurt, are you okay Sophia?'

'There is blood on the floor downstairs and the keypad has some on it too.'

'Don't worry.'

'What's going on? Why? Whose blood is it? Has he been back here while I was out?'

'Sophia, calm down, I am not to tell you, but…'

'Tell me what, what's going on?'

'Okay, first, everything is fine, later people are coming here. A man was shot.'

'Who?'

'He's coming here, is Adam's friend. Okay, you can trust his people.'

'And Adam is okay?'

'He almost got shot too.'

'What the... no, nobody is coming here, I'm putting a stop to this.'

'He will fire me for telling you, but you are safe, so is he. His friends are safe here, we are armed to protect.'

'José we are not on some fucking film set, this is real life! I want to know exactly what's going on, how do I get to where he is? There is a car full of shopping and I can't, I can't lose him.'

I fall to my feet, oranges falling loosely all over the floor, crying. José has his arms around my shoulders. He takes the black circle out of my hand.

'He gets the shopping from the car, make some tea Sophia.'

'I'm having wine, and lots of it.'

'As you wish.'

'José wait, where are wine glasses?'

'Already in the cupboard, there. You relax, I bring everything in.'

'Fine.'

Getting up off the floor, I open the cupboard and see flutes, wine glasses, tumblers. I take a wine glass and look around for a corkscrew, something else I forgot. José enters, his arms full.

'In the drawer next to the sink.'

'Thanks José.'

Walking towards the bathroom I look out of the window to see all my new blue pots planted, nicely arranged and picturesque. Smiling with a sense of irrevocable trust in José, I wash my face, bind my hair in a bun, stretch my neck in a circular motion. He didn't leave me stranded, he's busy dealing with God knows what.

I look at my reflection - my eyes are puffy. Hmm, if important people are coming here then I need to sort out the food, get ready, hair, make-up. I got this!

CHAPTER 33

✦✦✦✦

Kenny is pointing a black Sauer P229 at the doors, arm wrapped in the pink polo, bare chest pounding, watching CCTV screens, eyes dilated. Maria pulls up in her white Mini Cooper with the roof down. She leaves the car, walks up the stairs, keys in the code, all as usual. She smells the flowers and presses the code for the main release for the concierge doors, looks down at the phone, presses the red button for any messages. There's only one:

'The flowers are a message, hope you like them.' The phone rings and she sees it's Kenny and bites her lip.

'Hello.'

'Lock the main doors Maria, get in here now.'

'Okay.' She presses the code and runs towards the door leading to Kenny's office, presses the tag, peers into the glass to see Kenny. The green light flashes, a buzzer sounds and she opens the door. Her eyes widen when she sees the gun pointing towards her.

'What, Ken, what happened?'

'Heard that message? You know the voice?'

'No.'

'Think harder.'

'I don't know, let me clean your arm, let me see.'

'Sit down.'

'Okay, what has happened, who did this?'

'Told you didn't I?'

'Ken, you know me, you know I have you in my heart, I am loyal. Please stop pointing that thing at me, you are scaring me.'

'The word is out by now. Potentially I am dead but nobody knows. That's what's going around, you know, rumours, ha!'

'Why are you laughing, this is very serious no?'

'Of course they know I got away, police arrived at the scene, no bodies. See, I told you they want me, they already took my little bruv, the fucking bastards.'

'You have to let me fix your arm, please.'

'Okay, you have to get a knife, bandages and shit from next door.'

'A knife, what for?'

'You'll have to dig out the bullet, what do you think for?'

'Oh shit.' She rubs her temple, blinking at him. The gun is now lying on the table.

'Okay, I'll get everything.'

Kenny listens to every move. The whole place is full of listening devices, if she calls anyone; he hears her muttering in Spanish, rustling through the cupboards. She gets iodine, a handful of bandages, tape, a couple of needles, stapler, white soluble dressings, several towels, a small sharp knife and scissors, puts everything into a bowl. She hisses through her gritted teeth, 'Bastards, I'll kill anyone who fucks with my Kenny, he knows I love him, he must know by now. He needs to give me a gun too, the flowers were the message they are after me too, well fuck you.'

Kenny watches her on a monitor. He smiles ruefully, watching her emerge from the gym, and presses the buzzer to let her back inside. Taking a chair and placing it by Kenny, she sits and unwraps the bloody pink T-shirt, wipes the iodine over the open wound, sees the bullet inside.

'You ready?'

'just get on with it.'

'Okay, this is sure going to hurt, wait, what if...'

'What?'

'What if I can't stop the blood, what if it is an artery?'

'Just cut it out.'

Taking the knife, breathing heavily, she opens the hole deeper. Blood oozes out.

'I see it, I need something to pull it out.'

'Tweezers, in my bathroom.' She fetches them.

'You'll have to sterilise them. Fuck it, just get the fucker out, I'm infected anyway.'

'Infected with what?'

'Poison, the family, we are all cursed.'

'Don't be silly.'

'It's true, we do bad, none of us have done a righteous thing.'

'Hush, take a big drink of that poison before I pull it out.'

'Maria...'

'Hush, take a breath.' Amazingly, she is able to grip the bullet with the tweezers and pull it straight out.

'Ah, fuck, *fuck!*'

'It's out.'

Kenny throws the rest of the glass of liquor over the gushing wound and screams.

'What did you do that for? I got this, Kenny!'

'To sterilise it.'

'Everything is sterilised.'

'Not the knife and tweezers', he gasps.

'How bad is it?'

'Let me concentrate. I'm going to close the hole with this needle, it'll pierce the skin but can't be as painful as before.'

'Fuck me, I don't know what's worse, your medical skills or taking out a bullet. Just do it.'

'Bite the towel and stop shouting at me, Kenny.'

The phone starts ringing, and he looks down to see

an English number. He spits out the towel and answers it.

'What's going on?' he screams.

'Jerry and Matt are in open waters, nobody gave a statement at the terrace, nothing else at the moment. Is the bullet out? You're coming to mine.'

'Ah fucking hurry up Maria. And Adam, I'm not leaving here.'

'We're coming for you.'

'I told you earlier, I'm not leaving here, shouldn't have left at all.'

'Close the gym, shut down the fight.'

'Can't do that.'

'Everyone knows you are the target. Shut the gym, we're coming for you, resume tomorrow. We have to have a meeting. My men are armed, we're bringing you and Maria to mine.'

'The flowers were a message. She's coming with us.'

'You cleaned up?'

'She's on it now. How long Adam?'

'An hour.'

'You said that an hour ago.'

CHAPTER 34

✦✦✦✦

Mick, Terence and I are sitting in the Piucaro restaurant; Terence is dressed casually, black shorts, white T-shirt, brown dreadlocks the length of his brow, big brown eyes, with a long light jacket as always to cover the piece at his back. He can blend in anywhere, a people person, and now he's playing the part of a gay skipper on the yacht. Mick's dressed like he's just stepped out of Savile Row as per, short brown hair, a tanned physique, more muscular than Terence. Acting the gay couple works just fine.

In the private dining room the table is set for sixteen, but just three of us are here going over plans. We're drinking still water, looking at pictures, videos of Jerry and Matt popping a magnum, bubbles spilling over the side of the yacht before heading into the Mediterranean. We can't get to Jerry, only Matt.

I'm listening to a microphone earpiece; a one-sided conversation and it keeps breaking up. 'We're paying five million each for these two, all expenses paid.' Matt King's voice. Uncertain who he's talking about earlier back at his villa.

We didn't get much, heard no conspiracy; did Jerry pop the champagne at the same time as the shootout, thinking he could finally take over, be the kingpin once and for all?

'We've got zilch. Kenny needs to bug the changing rooms. The fight has to be stopped, we need something to get the Spanish police to intervene, find proof of Jerry taking bets from high bidders, find out if the police are being paid etc?' Adam interjects.

Mick, Terry and I sit in silence watching holiday makers soak up the sun on the outside terraces, sipping rosé, eating fresh lobsters, oysters over ice, the waiters hovering to top up empty glasses.

'Guys, I've got something, it's Junior talking about the fight. Matt must have left his jacket in the villa. Shush, it's not that clear.' Adam whispers.

I'm listening to a youth's voice, boasting how he is going to kill Wright in the ring, laughing, singing his dad's praises. He says MGM's boss almost got killed, he's oblivious to who the hitmen were, then he's boasting about another fight in a few months. The conversation appears to be on the phone. I'm hearing Jack's name:

'The fucker, Jack's next on Jerry's list, training him up to fight a knockout champion.'

'We've got to get him, we have to do something fast.' I sigh out loud, banging my fist on the table.

'I'm out of my depth here.' Adam stands, pacing up and down.

'What are you thinking, Mick?'

'We go to the villa, bust Junior's kneecaps, spin the tables around.'

'CCTV Mickey boy?'

'Won't work.' Adam screeches.

'Why not?' Terence glares up at Adam.

'Got to let it happen,' Mick shouts. 'Listening to him isn't getting us anywhere, we have to bug the changing rooms. I'll do it when we go and get those two at the gym.'

'Mick, you're not dressed for the gym. No offence, let Adam do it.'

'All right, I'll go and get changed.'

'You are a bit overdressed to be honest.' Adam laughs.

'You said to meet here, I dressed for the occasion.'

'Acting classes really paid off, you do look and sound gay.' Terry laughs, showing his amazingly white teeth.

'That's what you're paying us for, undercover agents, ha!'

'Ok, go and get changed, we have to move. I'll take my car, and I'll order a limo from the yacht. I want you two bulletproof. Meet me at the gym in half an hour.'

Leaving fifty euros on the table, I walk to the car. I know that face, it's him.

'Oi Jack, come over here.'

'I know you, you're Rebecca's brother.'

'Yes I am. What are you doing here?'

'I quit my job, boxing now, training every day.'

'You want to come to a barbecue?'

Jack's looking over the dock, sees the yacht isn't there. He peers at his bike.

'Can I ride this there? Where is it?'

'You can leave it at the back of Piucaro, it'll be safe, I know the owner.'

'Yeah, I know them too, wait a sec.' He disappears around the back of the building, then returns, wiping his long blonde hair away from his forehead. He's wearing denim shorts, white socks, white running shoes, white vest.

'Where's this party, any lovely ladies?'

'Maybe one or two.'

'A party with one or two? No, I think I'll pass.'

'Oh, you'll love her.'

'Yeah, is she single then?'

'Why don't you see for yourself? There'll be others, it's not a threesome if that's what you're thinking.'

'Ha! You really aren't selling this party, man.'

'It's not a party, it's a barbecue. Perhaps you can start off the party, Jack.'

'Drinks? Ah wait, I better not, I'm on a strict diet. Sod

it, do you have champagne?'

'Oh, plenty.'

Text to Terry: *Change of plan, go and get Kenny, I'll let him know it's you two, then come straight to mine.*

Text to Kenny: *A black limo will be outside, they're armed, use your cameras. Mick will bug the rooms, they are bringing you to mine, Adam.*

Text to Sophia: *Jack is with me, we'll be there in ten x.*

'Whoa, you busy inviting people to this barbecue of yours?'

'Jack, yes, in a fashion, guess I am.'

Text from Kenny: *All bugged, the gym's staying open, someone else on reception and Maria's coming with me, plus I'm armed as well.*

CHAPTER 35

✦✦✦✦

There's an array of different bowls of edible art, pretty salads, sealed in the fridges. Plates of crackers with crème fraiche, black caviar on the other plates, crème fraiche with avocado and sprinkles of mint, sliced baguettes with butter, cucumber, crushed black pepper drizzled with olive oil and a dash of balsamic vinegar, oat bread sliced with crème fraiche and prawns. I'm filling up the ice buckets. José opens the champagne and wine, putting the bottles into their pretty silver stands. He winds the canopy out over the barbecue area, placing four stands of champagne at either side of the patio seating. He puts out the bowls of nuts and the food on the main table inside, placing the silver and white paper towels on the side. He puts fifteen petite round crystal plates behind the paper towels.

I pick up my clothes shoved next to the lift and shout at José, 'I'll be down in two minutes, is that everything?'

'Looks perfect, are you a chef?'

'Ha no, but I know how to put some nibbles together, thank you.'

Upstairs I noticed that Adam has been through his bag. He has left his cologne on the bed, and there's a speck of blood on the white carpet. I bite my lip, take my hair out of my bun and pull through it with my fingers. I add a light pink rouge to my cheeks and lips, rubbing together, rubbing my cheeks, so I'm not stuck with big pink cheeks. Then I grab my white shoes, put them gingerly on and look at my reflection. I press the button and the door opens. On my way down I see Jack with a flute of bubbly in his hand. He's shocked, eyes wide catching my gaze. I gape at his muscular body. He smiles at me and I smile back, waiting for the door to open. Adam's out on the patio, he walks inside.

'Hey Sophia, what are you doing here? So good to see you, come here, give me a hug. You look amazing by the way.'

'Jack, we are here for you.'

'Sophia, that's enough.'

'Adam, it's the truth.'

'Wait a minute, what the fuck's going on?'

'Sit down Jack, enjoy your drink.'

'You put something in it?'

'The thought did cross my mind.'

'Adam, now that is quite enough, look, you're in danger, we're here for you.'

'Sophia, let me handle this.'

'No, someone was shot and somebody shot at you earlier. Jack needs to know the truth, Adam.' I look at José with saddened eyes, glancing frowning, miming, 'I'm sorry.'

'Someone needs to tell me what the fuck is going on or I am out of here.'

'You're not going anywhere!' screams Kenny, walking in with Maria, Terry and Mick.

'You have a very pretty home. My name is Maria, and you are?'

'Sophia! Hello, welcome to our home. Wine or champagne?'

'Champagne please, Sophia. Lovely view.'

'Follow me.' I walk outside onto the patio. We drink champagne, I down my flute in one, pour myself another, and Maria does exactly the same. We start laughing, drowning out what they're saying inside.

'We are dressed the same!' I tell her.

'Yes but no problem, you'll see we all wear same things here, it's not that uncommon. You get used to it after a while.'

'I'll drink to that. Which one are you with?' Sophia whispers.

'The one with the patch on his arm, he is my boss. I love him very much. And you are with the tall…?'

'Yes, that one in the black T-shirt.'

'Okay let's get this baby started, barbecue?' Adam says out loud, he strolls out, heads towards the barbecue. He fires up the heat and closes the lid, then casually walks over to fill up our glasses.

'You two seem to be getting along. Babe, can I borrow you for a minute? Excuse us Maria.' He takes my arm and walks towards the stairs leading down to the pool, then takes me down the steps, holding my hand. He pulls me lovingly into his chest.

'You look amazing, better than her.'

'Is that so? How do you know her, and what happened today?'

'Never mind that. I almost ran you over earlier, that was you in the road wasn't it?'

'That was you speeding? I screamed 'idiot' at you!'

'Yes, you had every right, but I want you to be more careful out here.'

'So the barbecue is on now? And who are they and why were you shot at?'

'You will find out for yourself. She's in love with Kenny. Come and meet everyone, the food tastes amazing. You brilliant woman, I love you.'

'There's meat in the fridge over there, you know sausages and burgers and all that. Adam, about José, I made him tell me. I saw the blood, I was hysterical. Please don't fire him, he potted all my herbs for me, he is really nice, please don't!'

'Shush, I am not firing one of my best men, come and mingle.'

'Who is Kenny?'

'Owns the gym, he got shot in the arm.'

'And you?'

'Skimmed my shoulder.'

'Do you think Jerry is behind this?'

'A hundred percent.'

'What if you're wrong? We're in one of the most gang-controlled places on earth.'

'Perhaps we'll find out who tried to kill Kenny.'

'They tried to kill you too.'

'That's why we think it's Jerry.'

'Can we trust everyone?'

'Never, ever trust anyone.'

'And you?'

'You're my life, my world, my everything. Let's go talk to him, he's probably nervous we got him here with ill-intent.'

'Okay I got this.' He holds my hand walking up the stairs. Everybody is outside, Jack and Maria talking standing face to face with flutes in their hands, Kenny sitting opposite Mick and Terry holding up their flutes, whistling at us. José is pouring champagne into everyone's glasses.

'I'm flippin' Hank Marvin here.'

'Kenny, there's salad and stuff inside mate.'

'Yeah well I am not some bunny rabbit am I?'

'I think it's hot enough now. Who's doing the bread here? Someone pass me a glass, I'm parched.'

'I'll do it.' Jack leaves Maria and walks over to the bar area. 'Here's your drink Adam, where's the knives and butter?'

'Inside. You spoke to her yet? You sort of should, she's the reason we're here for you, she's inside somewhere.' He points with his forefinger. 'On you go then.' Adam winks at José to follow, tilting his head inside.

'Whoa, you going to burn the fuck out of them sausages.'

'Shut it Terry. You want yours like you, crispy?'

'Ha ha, you got me there.'

'We got steaks too, who wants one?'

'Me.'

'Yeah, go on then bruv.'

'Me too.'

'How do you want them?'

'Bloody.'

'You animals. Right Maria, you?'

'No for me, I go inside bring the rest of food out, yes?'

'You angel. Bring those caviar things.'

'Kenny, you are obsessed with caviar.'

'Well I don't get out much, do I?'

'You would eat it out of the jar.'

'Ha, she knows me too well.'

Steaks sizzling away, smoke blowing in Adam's face with a gust of wind blinding him. He is not hearing the conversations. He places the steaks on the top level, cooked medium to almost rare, still not ready to be served.

'Right, burgers going on, I'm going inside. Terry turn them over, the sausages, where is everyone?'

'Probably getting away from your cooking skills.'

'Ha, well you're in charge, one minute.'

Picking up the plates, Maria takes them out. She walks up the stairs, listens to Sophia talking to Jack, José in the kitchen with them.

'Jack, the night you were in his car, he killed his wife. I bet he put you on a plane the next day offering you a new career, right?'

'What? How do you know this?'

'You understand now Jack? We're here for you. He killed his wife, I got arrested and almost framed for it, so did Adam.'

Adam appears. 'Come on out, the food's almost done. Did you get the cutlery, and that thing called butter?'

'Two minutes Adam, please.'

'Hurry up, we can fill in the gaps later on.'

'Jack go, you relax, I'll butter the bread rolls.'

'Hooray, come on Jack, we can eat, get hammered, who knows even take a dip in the pool. Let's get this party started. Jack, I know she's a little older, but Maria?'

'Ha, are you setting me up with her?'

'No way, just I know I would.'

'I heard that!' Sophia shouts up to Adam and Jack.

'Come on, you'll see we're telling the truth about the rigged boxing fight and Wright getting knocked down by King. You have to believe us, we have your back, we're trying to save you.'

'Yeah, well you just tell me what I've got to do, and after Saturday, if that happens like you say it will, I'll do whatever you want me to, all right?'

Maria is opening jars of ketchup, wholegrain mustard, caviar. The bread rolls are stacked on a silver tray on the bar counter so they can help themselves. Everyone's moving around, joining in together, mingling around the music on the surround sound. Tucking in, putting empty plates on the tables.

'José, unwind it mate.'

'No, leave it up.'

'Babe, we've eaten now, who's coming for a swim?' Adam takes another bottle out of the fridge and a champagne stand in the other and walks down the stairs, sitting on the blue fabric and standing back up again.

'Ah you fucker.' Kenny's in tow, laughing. Adam jumps in the pool fully clothed. Sophia bends over, leaning on the white concrete with Maria watching. Kenny jumps in too. Jack, Mick and Terry get up holding their glasses, walk down to the commotion, guns showing behind their shorts.

'Oh my.'

'You're okay here Sophia, nobody knows we are here.'

'How can you be so sure?'

'We weren't followed, that's how I know. Swim?'

'No, I'll clean up all of this.'

'I help, okay?' José takes another stand filled with an ice bucket, walks down to the pool and unwinds three umbrellas, placing the bucket underneath one.

'José, bring two more.'

'Yes sir.' Jack and Terry sit side by side underneath the umbrella, Jack's denim shorts dripping, sticking to his thighs.

Jack asks, 'You aren't going in? You're on the yacht next to ours, right?'

'We are watching you, making sure Jerry is taking care of you.'

'You been watching us for 24 hours?'

'Yeah, Jerry's keeping you out of everything it seems. You're eating chicken, tuna and rice every two hours, egg whites, every ten minutes we've seen that. He's training you up good, how many fights you had son?'

'None, I've been sparring in the ring with Matty the coach. You bugged me, the yacht?'

'Can't get to you, no we haven't.'

'How do you know all that?'

'By watching you. You don't exactly stay hidden, you're on the deck soaking in the sun and the woman comes out giving you more food and water. You're on a strict training diet all right, are they injecting you?'

'Steroid shit, yeah. He said he will pay me a million for the fight.'

'I know mate, but he'll make ten if not twenty out of you.'

'The bastard! It's doing my head in. How can I go back knowing what I know? Ah man, I just know I'm being set up now. I heard him on the phone saying I would be with Junior King on my first fight.'

'You can't say anything, you have to act normal. Matt's on the yacht now with Jerry, probably arranging your rigged fight. You do know Junior is a heavyweight? Look Jack, it would take two years of training to get up to that standard. If he puts you in a fight, it won't be public, it will be for all the mafia, the Colombians, you listening?'

Terry is on a mission to keep Jack's attention, because Mick is busy inserting transparent bugs in the souls of his white running shoes.

CHAPTER 36

✦✦✦✦

I'm sipping a gin and tonic, reading a book and lying underneath the umbrella, while Adam on the bed next to me is on the phone to someone who sounds like Mick. I listen in, surprised he's taking the call next to me. He winks at me, strokes my arm, holds my hand.

I mime, 'what's he saying?'

'Terry's been offered training in the ring to fight with Jack.'

'What?'

'Mick said he was having a beer on his yacht, saw Jack getting off his bike and walked in on them hearing Jerry offering to train Terry at his gym.'

'Jerry has a gym here too?'

'Don't think so.'

'I need to call Elaine.'

'Who?'

'Elaine the accountant. Word is she's doing my job as well, she will know where his gym is.'

'Wait a minute, can you trust her?'

'No! Not anyone, remember.'

'Don't call her. I've just had an idea of how to get me out of this mess.'

'Go on.'

'We get Jack to confess he was with Jerry, in his car, you know, probe him. Mick and Terry said he heard Jerry offering to train him in his gym, but he hasn't got a gym, he's trying to get Kenny out so he can get the gym. We need Jack here, get it all on tape. The police are looking for him, the missing piece of the puzzle.'

'You're amazing! But one thing you have to remember.'

'And that is?'

'DC Williams is leading the investigation and he's Jerry's best friend.'

'Ok we go to someone else, send over to Gary, we have friends in the force too remember.'

Phone beeps: Adam walks off, walking around the pool. 'He's where? But the fight's tomorrow, where's Jack? Ring Terry, tell him to bring him here.'

'What's happening?'

'Jerry's at the airport going back to London, the slimy fucker. Staying out of it I bet, so he isn't around when the kid goes down.'

'I'm pretty sure he'll be back for tomorrow.'

'No chance.'

'How can you be so certain he won't?'

'He doesn't want to get his hands dirty does he? He was never there, and nobody knows he is orchestrating it.'

'Adam, you're not thinking clearly. Come and sit down. What about all the people placing bets, the high rollers? Who's taking the bets, the money?'

'Jerry is, off the high rollers, but they're all criminals themselves. The bookies and Kenny are being paid off by Jerry after the fight.'

'Kenny won't get paid if he...'

'Yes babe, I know. You get Jack to confess, record him on your phone, I'm going out.'

'I think it's best if you do it, to be honest.'

'Terry will have a gun to his head, you need to do it. You can, and I have to go. I love you.'

'I love you, be careful.' I scratch my head, arms stretching in the air, and down the drink in one. Leaving everything on the table, I head to the main kitchen, open a bottle of wine and pour a large one. Then I prepare a large bowl of king prawn salad. Nibbling on celery, I take out the oat biscuits and put together a small array of nibbles, placing them neatly on plates, nuts in a bowl.

José pops his head in. 'Another party?'

'Hey José no, just a few friends coming.'

'You need help?'

'No, but you're so kind, thank you.'

'You know where I am if you need me.'

I carry the contents up the three stairs and place them on the table, then walk back to get my bottle. I pick out some paper napkins, three plates and cutlery, then walk back up to set the table. I get a bag of ice out of the freezer and open a bottle of champagne, putting it in the silver stand at the side. No gun at his head, no fucking way. I sit biting the skin on the side of my thumb, waiting with anticipation, panicking... over what? How am I going to get him to confess?

I button up my long white linen skirt and look around for my phone, then hear a car drive up. Hurriedly scouring for my phone, I run back to the kitchen and up the stairs and open the glass doors, leaving them flung open. I step down the stairs towards the pool, pick up my book and reach for my iPhone. I run back upstairs in the nick of time and sit down to see José down the hallway letting Jack and Terry inside.

Terry speaks first. 'You started early.'

'Nice to see you both. Drink?'

'You got a beer?'

'Yes, in the outside fridge at the bar, wait I'll get one. Jack?'

'I'll have some of that bubbly, where's the glasses?'

'Up there.'

'I'll get myself a beer. No, sit please, I know where they are.'

'Jack, one for me too please.'

'What are we celebrating?'

'Friendship?'

'Ha! Cheers friend.'

'Cheers Jack.'

'Sophia, I believe you, I just put two and two together. He's gone back to London, saying he's got to run his business, you know, keep it running smoothly. He mentioned you.'

'What did he say?'

'He said nobody ran his company like you, and Elaine is running his business into the ground, that kind of shit. He started singing too, the prick, you were right.'

'Was he singing 'What a Wonderful World', by Louis Armstrong?'

'Who is Louis Armstrong?'

'The fucking singer, bruv!' Terry screams, sipping his beer at the other end of the table. He puts his gun beside his can.

'You got that song Sophia, on Echo?'

'Terry, I don't know, YouTube it. Can you please put that gun away?'

'I flaming love that song.'

'No man, don't play it, reminds me of that prick setting me up. You going to the fight tomorrow night?' says Jack. I'm almost spitting my champagne out, my eyes wide. Terry laughs, showing his immaculate white teeth. He looks back at Jack swallowing the contents and laughs in his face. 'What?'

'Jack, I am not going to watch a young man die, and in a few months, it will be you.'

'I don't know what to do, how to get out of this. He's only giving me a hundred euros a week, says I'll get my million after one fight.'

'Jack, you're talented, you wanted my role, remember?'

'No, I wanted the promotion and you did it, then I ended up with a better proposition, and that's never going to fucking happen.'

'Excuse me, I need the ladies' room. Jack, help yourself to some king prawn salad, champagne too, you too Terry.'

'Very kind of you. Adam picked a winner with you, landed right on his feet, if you ask me.'

'Yeah she is something, isn't she?'

'Eyes and hands off Jack, you got no chance.'

In the ladies' I sit on the porcelain and hold my phone nervously, tapping for the recording app and pressing. I look at my Rolex, seeing how long the recording app lasts for. Come on, how long? I stop the app and ask Siri, whispering 'how long does the recording app last for?' Louder than expected, Siri answers, 'the recording app lasts whilst your phone is on, you may stop the recording at any time you like.' Fuck, so loud! Ruffling my curls, I walk out and head next door to José's room, knocking softly.

'José, did you hear that?'

'Hear what?'

'Ah, nothing.'

'Everything ok?'

'Yes, really sorry to bother you, see you later.' I gingerly shut his door and walk back down the hallway, confidently pressing the record app while pretending I am messaging someone. I place the phone on the table upside down and listen.

'Nice, this salad with the champagne.'

'Jack you just ate the prawns bruv, ha don't lie.'

'Come on, I know salads aren't a man's best thing, but it's all I got until I go out shopping. Jack, I need to ask you a question and I want you to be honest with me. My life is in danger.'

'Is that why you're here? Seems everyone's life is fucked over here.'

'Remember the night Jerry took you in his car?'

'You mean the night before he brought me here?'

'When was that, the Saturday, right? Why were you in his car Friday night?'

'I was pretty wasted. Jerry picked me up seeing me stamping home, said he would drive me home.'

'Did he?'

'Yeah.'

'What time?'

'Well, we stopped at his house but he told me to wait in the car, I don't know.'

'Think Jack, please.'

'Well, I think I left about an hour after you, I don't

know. It was still lightish, I think.'

'How long was he at his house for?'

'Don't know – about ten minutes.'

'Did you notice anything in the car?'

'No – yeah, he took his jumper out with him.'

'What colour was it?'

'I don't fucking know! Brown or blue.'

'Which?'

'Blue. What's with all the questions, and why is your life in danger?'

'Where did you go afterwards?'

'To the Castle for a drink. He asked if I wanted one, said it was on him. Course I said yeah.'

'What did he drink?'

'He ordered a double scotch, got me one too, nasty shit that stuff.'

'OK Jack thank you, thank you so much. Excuse me a second.'

Taking my phone, I walk down into the kitchen, pressing the sound down, listening to the whole conversation, sighing with relief.

Text to Adam: *Done x.*

CHAPTER 37

✦✦✦✦

'You got anything?'

'Nada.' Kenny draws on a cigarette.

'Why are you smoking again?'

'Because, Adam, in case you've forgotten, I got shot the other day.'

'Yah, it could have been worse, you could be in a coffin, me as well.'

'I don't want a lecture and it's my office. Drink?'

'Go on then, pass me a cigarette too.'

'Here, knock yourself out.'

'We have to stop the fight.'

'No can do, bets are rolling into my bookies. We're in the quarter of a million already and waiting for the mega money.'

'He won't pay you, wants everything you own.'

'I've got people on to him, he isn't going to touch a hair on my head.'

'What's left of it. Why don't you just shave those side bits? I mean, at least they're short but fuck me Kenny, you're bald, shave your bits off. He's gone to London.'

'London, yeah I know. Quite like my little stubble, thank you very much.'

'The gym's full, is Matt in?'

'Yeah. Listen in, it's on twenty-four seven and spins over. I've played back all of yesterday, not a word.'

'It's getting closer, he isn't going to slip up now.'

'It's stuffy in here. You coming out for a drink with me?'

'In your fucking dreams mate, not after the other day. Someone's watching me, I'm watching them.'

'Fuck sake Ken, what are you going to do after the fight, live in here? You can't live in fear. Plus, he can't give orders in a plane, can he?'

'It's my head or his, that's it, that's how it is.'

'Come to mine then.'

'No, fuck it, let's go out somewhere nice, late afternoon lunch on me.'

'Ken, it's almost night-time. Fuck me, you changed your mind quick, where do you want to go?'

'Where every fucker can see me, that's where. Let's go to my Buenos Aires, a nice bloody steak, I'll follow you in my Bentley, least that's bullet proof.'

'Not if they use an Era rocket launcher on you.'

'Ha ha. You want me out, let's go.'

'Ok, I'll follow you.'

'See you there.'

'Oh, and hurry up.'

'Be two minutes.'

Text to Sophia: *don't cook, I'll bring you something later, A x.*

Sophia: *I really think we should go back to London x.*

Adam: *Why and when? x.*

Sophia: *We have a confession and we have what we came for x.*

Adam: *We need him to come back with us, offer him a job before they leave x.*

Sophia: *They left x.*

Terry and Jack are sitting at the back where the sizzlers are, holding up their pints of beer in the air as Kenny and Adam approach. The waitress is already putting a bucket on the bar, throwing ice in, taking a magnum of Dom Perignon, walking over with four iced flutes. She knows what the King wants, he always orders the same in his restaurants.

'Blimey, this place is awesome man.'

'It's his.'

'No way!'

Adam sits down next to Jack. 'Jack, you're in danger now.'

'Me, why?'

'You're with us, people watching, Jerry will know as soon as he lands. I would like to offer you a job.'

'Here?'

'No, back in the UK.'

'What kind of job?'

'I don't know yet. Sophia said you're good at writing, you type fast.'

'Yeah, and?'

'You'll be on a good salary working for me.'

'How much?'

'I'll double what you were on back in England, how about that?'

'Fuck me, can I have that in writing?'

'When the contract is drawn up, yes. Get your passport and things off the yacht, Terry will go with you. Act gay.'

'No chance!' Jack laughs.

'I do it.' Terry giggles.

'Terry, no offence, but you look the part the way you dress.'

'Hey Jack, leave my shorts alone! Say what you want about me, but shorts, no man, you overstepped the line there bruv. Come on, let's go and get your stuff.'

We tuck into our steaks, heads down but eyes on the swivel watching everyone watching us.

Mick strolls in. 'Pass the champers. What a long fucking day.'

'Think you'd better tail Terry, he's with the kid. Take

them back to mine, get a take-away for you all, Sophia and José too.'

'What does she like?'

'Just get loads of different things, pretty sure she'll be happy with some.'

Mick downs his flute. 'I'm on it.'

CHAPTER 38

✦✦✦✦

Terry's on the yacht, watching Jack through binoculars. He sees a middle-aged woman with short grey hair chatting to him, passing him a plastic box. She leaves, walking off the jetty. Jack is changing clothes, donning a black string vest and blue denims, stuffing clothes into his rucksack.

'Come on Jack, hurry up you idiot.' Terry puts down the binoculars, leaves the galley and hops onto the jetty. 'What's that?'

Jack takes an egg and hands the plastic box full of hard-boiled eggs to Terry.

'She's just told me there is enough chicken and tuna and all these, enough to last until she comes back on Tuesday.' Terry chucks them all into the sea. They walk off the jetty, and Jack turns to face the yachts and the sunset.

'We got to go, Jack.'

'Going to really miss this, it's fucking beautiful.'

'Jack, get down, now!

But the shot hits Jack and he falls to the floor. Terry opens fire as the two masked men turn around, speeding off on their bikes towards the cars. Mick, approaching from the car, fires simultaneously. People are in silence, fleeing with fear. Terry pulls Jack, screaming, over his shoulder.

'I've got you, stay with me, I've got you son. Mick, you got here just in time, get his bag, he's been shot.'

'Where?'

'I don't fucking know, get him in the car quick!'

They lay him on the back seat, blood pouring from his back.

'That looks nasty.'

'I can't feel anything,' moans Jack.

'Mick, get us out of here. You're going to be okay Jack; it isn't near any organs.'

'How do you know?' Mick screams.

'I studied anatomy, didn't I?' He puts a towel over the wound and rolls Jack over on to his back.

'What did you turn him over for?'

'To keep pressure on the wound, Mickey.'

Mick shakes his head, he's driving as fast as he can, checking he's not being tailed. He dials Adam. 'Jack's been shot.'

'Don't take him to hospital, how bad is he?'

'He's alive, Terry says it isn't near any organs, he'll be okay.'

'Take him to mine, see you up there.'

'Who's been shot?' Kenny whispers over to Adam.

'Jack.'

'Is your mrs a nurse?'

'No.'

'Then how you going to take care of him?'

'I don't know.'

'I got a suggestion.'

'Spit it out then, we have to go.'

'The gym's closed now, we go there, get some first aid kit and shit.'

'You go and get it.'

'Come on, I know I've got a gun with me but fuck's sake, we're safer in your car. Leave mine here so people think I am still around. Fuck me, I thought you were the brainy one.'

'I'm a barrister, not a criminal fucking mastermind like you.'

'Come on Adam, we're taking your car, you drive, I'll shoot.'

'Oh for fuck's sake, let's go.'

'One minute.' Kenny walks over to the waitress, whispers into her ear, signals for Adam to go over to them. Ken opens a door; they walk through and close the door.

'What are we doing in your conference room?'

'Letting everyone know we're having a fucking conference. Come on, your car is the other side of this door, see, up here for using your nut.' He jabs his head.

Jack's eyes start closing, his breath slowing down, chest getting slower with each inhale.

'Jack, open your eyes, stay with me, you're going to be okay, you are listening?'

'He needs a hospital Terry, what if his lungs are collapsing?'

'It's too high up, near his shoulder.'

'Are you fucking sure?'

'Of course I'm sure, it's just, well, shock. Jack, open your eyes, look at me.'

'He's losing it.'

'Is he fuck, it's shock.'

'The lungs are near the shoulder.'

José runs out of the door, hearing the car. Mick and Terry carry Jack and lay him on the kitchen table face down. He looks unconscious.

Upstairs, after taking a long soak in the tub, Sophia is watching the sun set with a glass of wine in her hand, smiling at the prettiness of the scene. Hearing voices, she slips on a cream silk nightdress and matching robe, puts on her cream Ugg slippers and runs down the hall, down the stairs.

'Hello, Adam, are you home?'

She looks down the hallway to see José, Mick and Terry around the table, blood spots on the floor. She gasps, clasps her hands around her face, screaming, 'Adam, no, no, no!'

'It's Jack.'

'Oh no, Jack, is he dead?'

'Got a pulse, think we're losing him though.'

'Oh, my poor Jack, let me see.'

'What happened, where's Adam, who is watching him, if you're all here? Has anything happened to him, where is he?'

José, walking back to his room speechless, pulls out a bag from his wardrobe and returns to the table. He opens the bag, takes out scissors and cuts the black vest. He gets out iodine and pours it over Jack's back, then removes the bullet with apparent ease. He staples the hole closed and puts on a patch. He gestures to Mick and they turn Jack over. José pierces a hole in Jack's chest and pushes a pipe into it. Blood pours out of the pipe. He injects Jack with a large dose of adrenaline. Jack's eyes are open wide. He's gasping for air, breaths out a huge gulp.

'Sit him up quick.'

'José, you're a fucking genius,' says Mick.

Sophia wipes away her tears. 'Jack, you're going to be okay,' she whispers.

'I could have done that if I had a bag like that.' Terry smiles at Jack. 'Told you you he'd be okay didn't I? He needs hospital soon.'

'José, how soon?' Sophia kisses his cheek.

Adam and Kenny rush in carrying a bag filled with towels and an assortment of first aid equipment. They see Jack sitting up, bloodshot eyes, tears roll down his face.

'Adam, José says he needs a hospital.'

'No chance, the police are waiting for anyone else who turns up shot.'

'But his lung has been pierced. José did everything, he saved his life, we have to get him to a hospital, and soon.'

CHAPTER 39

✦✦✦✦

MGM stadium; seats filling up, lights flashing over the ring and around the audience, loud music blasting *Carry On Regardless* by the Beautiful South, followed by *Nickel Back Rockstar* as the girls in the ring walk around in skimpy white shorts, white bikinis on their double-D breasts, long black shiny hair, tanned skin. One is holding up Wright's picture, the other has King's. The crowds are whistling.

Matt with Junior in one changing room, Jamie and Kim in the next, hearing the ambience of the crowds, music on the surround. Kim is punching into thin air as Jamie prepares him, tying the laces of his black boots: 'Oi keep still a minute, compose yourself, sit down. Right you're going to duck at every blow, always move your head from left to right. You got this, you can do this, you are listening?'

'Yes Jamie, I'm going to knock him right out, you'll see.'

'That's it son, that's it. Now don't let him anywhere near that eye, if you let him open that cheek again, you'll start doubting yourself, and doubt kills, you hear me?'

'Yes, I'm ready.'

'We got fifteen minutes yet. Now listen here son, remember he's the world champion and you're going to take the title off him.' Wright's looking into his reflection, black shiny skin, tattoos over his neck, skinhead, hissing through his teeth and bouncing up and down, moving his neck around. He's dancing and throwing punches with his black gloves on the red bag.

Meanwhile next door Matt is preparing his son, giving him a line of cocaine, getting his son ready to kill Wright.

'You want another?'

'Not yet dad, fucking hell, that's good, where did you get this?'

'You know me son.'

'Yeah, you're a mean fucker.'

'Like father, like son kid. I got the coke right off the Colombians, you haven't met them yet, but they're here son. We're all counting on you and I know you'll do what you're supposed to do.'

'Dad I don't want to kill him, can't I just knock him out?'

'Fucking hell, are you getting a conscience? Ten minutes before the fight?'

'It isn't right, is it?'

'Jerry wants you to kill him, that's why you're being paid so much. The cartel wants this as well. Don't back down, here, have another livener.'

He sniffs a line off the side mirror and looks at himself, big brown eyes. He scratches his dreadlocks, flexes his muscles, looks at his white shorts with his name on them written in pink, then at his gloves.

'Pink fucking gloves – dad, you serious?'

'It's a deterrent son. Now do your exercises, get yourself buzzed up.'

Matt puts the pink gloves on, fastening them tightly.

Next door, the referee, in black trousers and a blue shirt with a bow tie, walks into Jamie and Kim.

'You ready?'

'Ready as ever mate.'

Adam and Kenny are sitting in the office, clinking their crystal glasses together, eager to see what happens. They watch the screen on the glass pane, near the door.

Jamie puts a black silk robe around Kim. The music starts getting quieter and the trainers come in. The referee walks out into Matt and Junior, followed by their trainers, who put a pink robe around Junior. They're both in their rooms bouncing around as the commentator shouts over the Tannoy, 'Are you ready?'

The crowds start cheering and whistling as Junior

walks out dancing down the pathway towards the ring to a Rich Piana theme song. He's getting everyone excited, cheering for Junior King. The commentator introduces him. 'Here is the world's heavyweight champion, WBC winner by twelve knockouts, from the United States of America, it's Junior King!'

The audience stands up cheering for King. Junior shakes his head from side to side, and a trainer puts a rubber guard piece in his mouth.

Natty Anthem by Rich Piana plays as Kim Wright steps towards the ring. The commentator: 'Here he is with ten knockouts, heavyweight, straight from the United Kingdom, it's Kim Wright!'

The audience screams out, all shouting at the same time, 'Wright, Wright, Wright!' Someone shouts, 'we love you!' A trainer puts a rubber guard in Wright's mouth, and the fighters stare at each other from their corners of the ring. Matt's holding up the gold belt behind his son's head, trying to put Wright off. Both walk centre stage, eyes locked onto each other, the referee at the side of them.

The whistle blows.

'Junior tries to punch Kim, he misses the blow, ooh, Kim a right cross to Junior's head, and another jab in his body, there he goes. Another two crosses to Junior's head, whoa one more, Junior falls to the floor, oh this is good!'

The audience stands up, cheering for Wright. The referee asks, 'you all right, can you get up?' Junior nods, the whistle blows and they both head back to their corners, wet towels over their shoulders, then dry off. Wright spits his guard out, takes a drink of water and spits it out. The commentator's saying, 'this has to be frustrating for Junior now, can he make a comeback, is he going to pull it off? I think he can. What's in his mind right now? That was an epic first round by Kim Wright.'

'What the fuck was that, son?'

'Dad, I got this.'

'You go and knock him down in one son, just hit a blow on his head, the left. He's expecting you to use your right hand, like in training. He's thinking about your move. You think harder, now go get him.'

The audience sits back down as the bells ring, the referee's centre stage, moving out of the way as Junior dances over. Kim stands up, walking over and Junior knocks him with one straight left hook to his head. 'Whoa Junior King is making a comeback everybody, Wright's knocked down, will he get up?'

The audience is cheering, screaming 'King, King, King, yes, yes, yes!'

'He's up' says the commentator. 'Can Wright pull it together? Junior's walking over, oh here we go now folks, ooh a double cross blow to Kim's body, he's covering his head, oh and another left hook trying to get to Wright's head.' The bell rings. 'What's Kim doing? Wright carries on punching King's head as he walks to his seat. The referee intervenes as Junior turns around throwing a punch into the air.

'Great performance there by King everyone, this fight is good.' The audience all clap, cheer and whistle.

The fighters are being patted down, both being screamed at by their coaches. Wright nods to Jamie, putting his rubber guard back in his mouth. The bells ring and he dances into centre stage, moving away from Junior's fists, they're staring at each other. 'Here we go now, Wright's dodging every cross King throws, what's Wright doing? Whoa, a double cross into Junior King's head, Wright's not stopping now, and another, whoa a double right hook into his head, Juniors down! Will he get up? This is an amazing fight, but will Junior King get up?'

Kim's dancing on his feet waiting to attack as Junior stumbles up, his dad on the side screaming at him The referee counts down: 'ten, nine, eight, seven, six, five, four, three, two'. Junior tries, but he can only hold onto the rail. The crowd's jumping up and down screaming 'Wright, Wright, Wright, yeah!' Those with ringside seats frown, shaking their heads.

'The new WBC heavyweight champions is... It is Mr Kim Wright everybody! That was intense, a new world record, in one minute and seven seconds, that's the fastest on record. Whoa, we have a new champion! What's this?' Just as Jamie hands the gold title to Kim in the ring, Junior gets up and walks over to hug him. The audience all quieten down, and some are leaving their seats. Some still chant Wright's name, some are whistling. Armed police have ambushed the arena and they are handcuffing Matt, then Junior. The audience is watching eyes, wide. The cartel men are gone, fleeing out of the side doors.

CHAPTER 40

✦✦✦✦

Virgen De La Victoria Hospital. In the private suite Jack is watching the fight on TV, while Sophia sits on a chair next to the bed. Mick sits outside with a coffee watching the screen through the glass. Spanish TV is showing the ambush. Jack sees the men from the two cartels fleeing the front row seats. They had been on the yacht a couple of days ago.

Jerry orders Jack to take a bike ride for a while, not to come back until night time. He's shaking his head.

Sophia looks at Jack. 'Are you okay?'

'Yeah, you?'

'What's on your mind?'

'That fight, why did it get ambushed like that?'

'I really don't know, Jack.'

'It's down to Adam I reckon.'

'Perhaps.'

'He's clever.'

'Are you going to take the job he offered you?'

'Fuck yeah, he's paying me double what you offered me.'

'Ha! Well, I may fight you for the role.'

'You better fucking not.'

'Watch your language! The job's yours.'

'And how do I know you won't steal if from me?'

'You don't.'

'See, we're still fighting for a position and I bet he gives it you.'

'Jack, he's already given it you, I'll be looking somewhere else I promise you. You're looking a lot better, do you want another cup of tea?'

'No, it's horrible in here. Wouldn't mind an orange juice and a sandwich.'

'What kind of sandwich?'

'Whatever they have, but not chicken or tuna please.'

'Cheese and ham?'

'Yeah, definitely, can you toast it?'

'I'll ask, see what I can do.'

Adam's sitting next to Ken sipping bourbon, laughing, pressing rewind, listening to Matt and Junior's conversation in the changing room. They clash the crystal together.

'We fucking did it, Kenny.'

'Well, I'm not getting paid, that's for sure, I'm going to have to go back to the UK. There's going to be a number of hits on me now for snitching.'

'I can get you back, but there's only room for five. I'll have to send for you after I get them back.'

'When are you going?'

'Tonight.'

'How are you going to clear the airspace at these hours?'

'Fuck, is that the time? I lost track, I have to go now, you going to be okay?'

'Got this haven't I. No fucker can get in here anyway.'

Text to Terry: *pick me up now.*

Terry pulls up outside the gym in the silver Lamborghini, the side door automatically opens for Adam and closes as he gets into the seat. They speed off.

'That fight, fuck me, it was amazing watching that inside the stadium.

'Didn't know it would turn out like that, I was pretty sure Wright was going to get killed.'

'Me too, what the fuck were the police there for, who snitched?'

'I don't know.'

'Was it you?'

'Don't be stupid, Terry. We're leaving, all of us, tonight.'

'Oh, how do you propose that?'

'Helicopter.'

'A fucking helicopter, tonight?'

'That's what I said.'

'Who, all of us? How many does it fit, they're only designed for three, maybe four, there's five of us.'

'Terry, you're smart.'

'Yeah, I am aren't I, see, I told you.'

'Five.'

'Five what?'

'The helicopter fits five, two in the front, three in the back.'

'Oh, but you're missing something bruv.'

'And that is?'

'The pilot, that makes six. So who's staying behind, I know, shotgun?'

'Ha, you will be in the back.'

'No mate, I want the front seat. Where we driving to, the villa?'

'No, I'll type it in, there, that's where.'

'You did the right thing by the kid, is he out of surgery?'

'Yes, he's fit to leave.'

'Who's being left? Let Mick stay.'

'Terry, I am flying and I can't have you in the front, won't be able to concentrate with you rambling on.'

'You?'

'Yes.'

'You can fly? Got a licence?'

'Yes, I have a licence.'

'You got a helicopter waiting at the hospital?'

'Not yet.'

'Then how are we...'

'Stop with all the questions, I'll arrange everything.'

'With who? Are you just going to ask the hospital if you can borrow theirs?'

'Can you wire it?'

'So that's it then, we're just going to steal a helicopter?'

'If we have to. Well, technically, you're stealing it.'

'Fucking yes bruv.'

'I'm winding you up, knew you would get a kick out of that.'

'Ah man, you're putting me on a downer. How are we going to get a helicopter?'

CHAPTER 41

✦✦✦✦

Kenny is blinking at the CCTV; eyes closing, prising them open, not wanting to miss if anyone tries to break in, sipping the bourbon, emptying the decanter. The leather chair is comfortable and he doesn't want to leave it, but he rises anyway and opens the cupboard door. He takes out a Gigondas 2011, twists the corkscrew, bites off the cork and spits it out across the table, still staring at the screens. He pours it into the crystal and takes a swig of the ruby-red wine. Come on then, try and get in here you fuckers, I know you're out there. Well I am the master, you got that? He pours another full glass. I'm not going to sleep, not a chance.

The phone rings; he almost jumps out of the chair at the sound, stands on uneasy legs, looking at the screen.

Maria calling. Ah fuck, what does she want? Fuck it, I'm not answering. He sits back down and it rings again. He looks at her name, looks back at the screens, gulps back the wine in one, rubs his eyes and fills up his glass once more.

The phone is flashing again. Fuck off, you silly bitch! Holy fuck, what if she's in danger, if someone's got a gun to her head? Nothing I can do about it. He's breathing faster, freaking out, perspiration running down his chest. The telephone flashes again. He's going to have to answer it.

'What?'

'I can hear you, Ken.'

'How can you fucking hear me, are you here?'

'No, he gave me an earpiece.'

'Who?'

'Adam. Said to call you if you go insane and I think you are getting crazy.'

'Oh really, the fucking pig bugged me?'

'Said it's for your own good.'

'Maria, I am fine. What a twat.'

'Who? me?'

'No, Adam, the fucker.'

'I come to stay with you, si?'

'You're not safe, stay in the apartment.'

'Ken, I am safe, Mick gave me a gun and showed me how to use it.'

'No, smart arse, stay inside, they're going to get you

if you leave.'

'No one is outside, I can see from cameras, up and down the street, I can move the mouse, it is so cool, I see everywhere around, nobody here.'

'Well stay there and play with it.'

'I want to be with you, no one has gun to my head.'

'How do I know that?'

'You believe me, trust?'

'No, I'm not buying it.'

'Kenny I love you, you know that?'

'Maria, just stay in your apartment, I'll get someone to pick you up tomorrow.'

'You will not sleep, your insomnia will come back, I know you.'

'Maria, I'm fine.'

'You drink, still won't sleep, let me come, I promise to look after you.'

'No, I said no!'

Maria throws her denim jacket over her shoulders and ties the arms around her collarbone. She's wearing a black knee-length velvet dress, black and red Louis Vuitton heels. She puts clothes into her Gucci case, deodorants, perfumes, make up bag, hair accessories and her Jimmy Choos. She frees her hair, sprays on a dash of Victoria's Secret lavish oil, runs her fingers through it. 'I am coming whether you want me to or not, silly gay man, I'll change you, I can change you.' Not checking the laptop, she picks up her bag, grabs her keys and leaves. She presses the elevator button. 'Venga, come on, come on!' The silver door quietly beeps, she steps inside, presses the button and stands watching the screen: 10, 9, 8, 7, 6, 5, 4, 3, 2, 1. The door opens and she walks through the concierge doors, pressing the key. The car lights flash, she places her bag in the back, gets into the front and drives off.

She dials his phone. 'Silly man, no one is watching me, I told you silly man.'

'Maria?'

'I am driving to you.'

'Go home.'

'No.'

'Fuck it! Fine, make sure you are not being followed.'

'Yes, I am sure.'

'You're a mad woman.'

'For you, yes. I'll do anything for you, you know this.'

He's watching the CCTV, sees her car pull up, smirking to himself. He watches her figure bending over to retrieve her bag. She walks up the stairs and keys in the code.

A masked man suddenly appears from the stairs, throws a black bag over her head. Others appear, brandishing guns.

Kenny's eyes widen as he watches the scene.

'Fuck, fuck, fucking hell, you stupid fuck, I am fucked!' He's watching Maria being dragged by a masked man. The man is screaming at her, 'Enter the code for the gym now!'

'I can't see, you stupid prick,' she sobs. He removes the bag from her head, points the gun.

'Enter the code.'

Her eyes widen as she feels the gun on her cheek, tears rolling down her face.

'Okay, please don't…'

'Shut it, enter the code to his office.'

'I can't, he keeps that to himself, I am not allowed inside.'

'Bullshit!'

'It's the truth, he is, you know…'

'What?'

'Gay.'

'Right, shut it. We're in. Come out Kenny or we'll blow you out.'

With only their eyes visible, they all stay covered, knowing the whole place is on camera. One takes a chair, throws her onto it, black tiebacks around her ankles and wrists, a grey mask over her mouth. He removes her denim jacket, runs a small machete around her breasts. Maria's eyes widen, she breathes faster, tears and snot from her nose mingling together.

Kenny can see her through the glass. He looks at her, knowing none of them can see him through the black bulletproof pane. He has his hand over his mouth.

'You stupid cow, they are going to kill you.'

'You can hear us, Kenny. Come out or I'll cut off her breasts with this.'

'Give me five minutes, I'm not dressed, you just woke me up you fuckers.'

'You got two minutes or we start cutting her into tiny pieces.'

He rushes around the back of his office, collects his gun, passport and a wad of euros, then opens the wardrobe door and flees through the back, leaving her in the hands of the hitmen. He knows she will soon be dead. He dials Jimbo.

'Oi, get to the gym, there are seven inside, they have Maria tied up. Get there now, shoot them. The code is 7422 2000, repeat it.'

'We're on it, 7422 2000.'

'How long?'

'Two, three at the most.'

'She'll be dead in five, fucking hurry up.'

He runs down a back street to an old banged-up blue Ford, jumps in and starts the engine. He looks up to see Jimbo driving up towards him, but Jimbo is pointing a gun at him. He fires and one bullet hits Kenny. His foot presses the accelerator and the car crashes into another, which in turn crashes forward into another. Alarms go off.

Over the speaker on a masked man's cufflinks, Maria hears the voice and screams, mouth open wide.

'It's done, I got him.'

'Where? Shut it bitch!'

'Out back, hear the alarms? Got his head, he's finished.'

'You two, go check the back.'

'You are one lucky bitch, I should finish you.' The man tears off her grey mask. Maria starts gasping for air,

'Fuck you.'

'You're one cheeky cow, I like that.' He slaps her across the face, points the gun at her head. 'You want to join him?'

'If you are going to do it, then fucking do it!'

CHAPTER 42

✦✦✦✦

José is hacking into the computer system, seeing and hearing everything. 'We have a code red, send the helicopter now.' He disconnects all the computers, grabs three bags, runs to the grassy knoll on the mountain and jumps into the black helicopter. Then he walks into the suite and hands over two bags.

'It is ready.'

'Thank you. Right, get dressed, we're leaving in two, Jack, quick!'

José passes Sophia a light bag. Inside she sees her passport and Chanel purse. Jack picks up his rucksack and opens the door, unsteady on his feet. José points to the back staircase.

'Sir, you have to go now.'

'Thanks.'

Sophia takes her seat in the front. Adam fastens her belt, puts on her H10-36 headset, turns a silver switch so he can hear only her, not wanting communication from the three in the back. He flicks the switch to the back for a minute.

'You ready?'

'Yes, this is fucking cool.'

'Jack, you won't be able to hear us in a minute, talk to those two.'

'10-4,' Mick shouts.

Terry looks at him. 'We aren't on fucking walkie talkies, Mick.'

They climb and begin to fly towards the airport. Sophia looks at Adam and he turns towards her glare, smiling and speaking into the side piece.

'You ok?'

'Yes. Are we flying all the way home in this?'

'No, we're going to the airport. See that light over there?'

'How are we going to, er...'

'What?'

'Be allowed to land, security and stuff.'

'It's all sorted and paid for, we are fine, taking the jet at 4am.'

'Wow, you are quite something.'

'Quite?'

'You're amazing.'

'So are you. We get him back, take him to Gary's, he can confess everything, and I'm a free man.'

'We did it.'

'We sure did.'

'Adam, your phone's ringing.'

'Leave it.'

'It's Maria.'

'Leave it.'

'She keeps ringing, Adam.'

'We're landing now, leave it.'

Moving around in the rear of the private jet, they watch Adam on the tarmac, phone at his ear, walking in circles.

'What's happening now, are we leaving or what?'

'Yes Jack, in about half an hour.'

'Why is he pacing around like that?'

Terry grunts. 'Something's up, that's why. Something's happened, that's what he does when he's worked up.'

'Fuck, what now?'

'I don't know Mickey, go out and ask him.'

'I will.' Sophia goes down the steps and walks towards Adam. He doesn't notice. He's putting his phone into his pocket, his back to the jet. Sophia holds his shoulders, gently turns him around, stares into his eyes.

'What is it?'

'That was Maria. It's Kenny, he's dead.'

'Oh no, oh Adam I am so sorry, how did it happen?'

'They got Maria, tied her up, he did a runner out the back, jumped in a car, someone drove by and shot him, that's all she knows, she's...'

'What? Is she safe, did they hurt her?'

'They let her go but she's in a state.'

'We have to help her, phone José, get him to get her, she can come with us maybe?'

'No, I'll make a few calls, you go and wait inside.'

'Adam.'

'Sophia, please.'

CHAPTER 43

✦✦✦✦

Danny is asleep, lying in bed in his white shorts, tanned, muscular physique, short brown hair, his wife at his side in a white linen nightdress, flowing black hair on the pillow. He wakes to the sound of his phone, leaves the bed scratching the back of his ear.

'What's up?'

'Kenny, he's...'

'He's what?'

'Sorry Danny, bad news, he's been shot in his car.'

Jimbo sounds tearful, but unseen, he has a smirk on his face; he's working for the other Kelly family now.

'No, no fucking way! I'm sending my other brothers down to sort this once and for all. Maria?'

'She's okay, they let her go.'

'I'm making arrangements, see you down there

tomorrow. We're on fucking holiday and you are being fucking paid to protect him for fuck's sake Jimbo! You are fucking dead, do you hear me?'

Danny hangs up and the baby starts crying. He walks into her room, picks her out of her crib, hugging her, smelling her nappy. 'Alena wake up, come in here.'

His wife, five foot two, skinny, olive skin, piercing inset blue eyes, is now out of bed and wearing her white linen robe. 'Don't know why you can't fucking do it, who was that?'

'They killed my brother.'

'Which one, oh my babe, oh no, I am so...'

'Kenny.'

'Oh, baby I am sorry, what are we going to do?'

'We're leaving Majorca today, going back to Madrid, leaving you and the baby at home, rounding up the other eight. We're going to sort the Kellys out once and for all, that's what we're going to do.'

'Baby, your phone is ringing.'

'Hello, what, who is this?'

'Jimbo shot him.' The phone cuts off.

'The fucking scumbag. I knew, I fucking told Ken not to trust him.'

'What's happened?'

'Nothing.'

'Danny, please tell me?'

'Alena, a woman, I know her voice but can't think of her name.'

'What did she say?'

'That fucking two-faced Jimbo shot him.'

'How do we know it's not a setup, why would he betray Ken?'

'Because, that voice, it's her.'

'Who?'

'Maria, it was her voice.' He's remembered now.

'Are you certain?'

'Yes, she wouldn't lie, would she?'

'Ring her back.'

'And say what?'

'I don't know, think.'

He dials Maria's number. 'Oi, why did you ring off a private number?'

'I'm scared, sorry, I am.'

'Who are you with?'

'Nobody, I'm in my apartment. They tied me up, threatened to cut off my boobs if he didn't come out of the office.'

'How do you know it was Jim?'

'I was there, heard his voice on the walkie-talkie thing.'

'What did he say?'

'Said he shot him in his car, it's done, he said.'

'The fucking Irish scumbag, what else do you know?'

'Ken told me that that Cockney in London orchestrated the fight, I don't know his name.'

'I fucking do.'

'Sorry Danny, that's all I know.'

'You going to be all right? Shall I send for someone to be with you?'

'No, I'm fine.'

'You don't sound fine. I can hear you're shaken up badly.'

'Danny, I just lost the man I love, I want to be alone.'

'Stop crying.'

'I can't.'

'Let me speak to her.'

'Alena wants to talk to you.'

Alena takes the phone, multitasking, changing the baby and consoling Maria. Danny takes another phone, an old black one, leaving Alena to talk to Maria. He makes several calls, wiping tears away as he tells his mum. He rounds up a meeting in Madrid, ordering his brother's body to be driven up, planning for the family to have a funeral back home in Ireland.

Two men sit opposite the apartment; one tall, muscular build, short blonde hair, brown eyes, dressed in denims and a white polo shirt. He watches Danny pacing around the apartment, listening in to the conversations, gun at his side but knowing he can't shoot in the resort complex. The other man is fat, jet-black hair, wearing a red polo shirt and black trousers. He stands drinking a beer, wanting and waiting to take him out.

CHAPTER 44

✦✦✦✦

We're flying back over the French Alps, Mick and Terry fast asleep, Jack wide awake, looking down at the mountains. Dawn has broken and the sun is on the horizon. Sophia is asleep in the front, head down resting on her chest. Opening her eyes, she tilts her head back onto the headrest, one hand on her belt. Her head lolls back down, then jolts back to the headrest. Her eyes are open wide now, it's pointless trying to sleep with the turbulence.

Looking ahead, she sees another plane higher up in the sky.

'Hey sleepyhead, you ok?'

'Uh, mm, yes, you?'

'Perfect, just a little turbulence. Try and sleep, still forty-five minutes to go.'

'No, I'm ok, just can't wait to get back home. The last few days, well, I'm mentally exhausted, aren't you?'

'I can't afford to be, got to get us home.'

'More coffee?'

'You read my mind.'

Undoing the seat belt, walking out of the cabin, she sees Mick and Terry sleeping, and looks at Jack looking at her.

'What are we going to do when we get back? Who am I going to stay with, am I going back to my parents' place?'

'If you want to, yes, why not?'

'So you're not kidnapping me?'

'Haha. No we aren't.'

'You sure?'

'Of course I'm sure.'

Terry stirs, wiping dribble from his mouth, looking over at the conversation. 'Any coffee going?'

Mick opens his eyes. 'What are you shouting for?'

'Wakey wakey Mr Sunshine.'

'It's over there Terry, make Adam and me one too please.'

'And me bruv.'

'Fucking hell, why do I get all the crap jobs?'

'It's what you're paid for.'

'Jack, do you want a coffee?'

'No, I don't drink it, I'll have a tea though please Terence.'

'Get up and make it yourself then.'

Terry hands two cups of coffee to Sophia and opens the cabin door for her. 'There you are love, you all right Captain?'

'Yes, shut the door.'

'Ten-four captain.' He closes the door, takes a coffee to Mick, looks at Jack, nods over to the drinks section.

'Go on son.'

'Why didn't you make him a cuppa?'

'Because he's not fucking disabled, is he Mick?'

'No, but the kid's been shot.'

'Oh, sit down son, I'll make you a cup of chai.'

'Thanks Terry.'

'Don't get used to it.'

'Jack asked if he can go back to his parents' house.'

'I heard.'

'Can he?'

'No.'

'Why not?'

'Because he isn't safe, he's only safe with us. We're going straight to Gary's and he's going to confess on video.'

'But the police might not accept that.'

'Then we take him to the station.'

'We need to make copies of the audio.'

'Already done.'

'Oh, when?'

'The minute you sent it to me.'

'You think of everything.'

'It's my job to.'

'When this is over, can we go back to our villa?'

'Whenever you wish, but not this year.'

'Why not?'

'It's complicated.'

'What's happening now?'

'There are two families caught up in criminal warfare and I am their barrister, that's why you can't go back.'

'And you are going?'

'It's my job, I have to.'

'Tell me about it.'

'You know I don't talk about my work.'

'I think I'm entitled to know what you're dealing with if you don't mind.'

'Ah, fine, you know too much already.'

'No, on the contrary, you haven't explained that much, you're like a...'

'Like a what?'

'A closed book sometimes, most of the time, in all honesty.'

'Kenny O'Connor has nine brothers. Well, there were ten, now there are eight. One sister too. They run half of Marbella, and I work for them.'

'Wow, their parents were busy. Go on.'

'The Kelly cartel run the other half. They bought ship containers, bringing in drugs from the Colombians... you sure you want to know the rest?'

'Oh yes.'

'so, the cartel wants the O'Connors out, they've been attacking each other's families for the last five years.'

'What if you get...'

'Don't worry, I keep a low profile.'

'But they know who you are?'

'Probably, yes'

'You could get killed.'

'No, they want the other family, I'm a nobody to them.'

'You got shot at.'

'It was Ken they wanted, not me, I was just in the wrong place at the right time.'

'You mean wrong time.'

'Well, I'm alive, I pulled Ken down, saved his... ah, the poor fucker.'

'I know, he was, seemed really nice.'

'He was just as bad as them, wasn't he?'

'Right you, enough. We're going to start descending in five minutes, can you get me another coffee quickly babe?'

Making the coffee, Sophia nearly jumps out of her skin hearing him. 'This is your captain speaking, ha ha, fasten your seatbelts, there isn't a sign, we're about to descend, no more drinks, thanks for flying with us today, it's been emotional.'

'You can fucking say that again bruv.'

All three start clapping and cheering. Sophia shakes

her head and smiles, returns to the cabin, places the coffee in the holder, sits down, fastens her seat belt and looks ahead towards the runway.

'Ready? Here we go.'

They land and pull onto the private area. Two limousines are waiting at the bay. A well-tailored man emerges from one of the cars, stands waiting. Nobody gets out of the other car. Sophia bites her lip nervously, thinking 'he's precocious all right, but who's in the other car?'

'Adam, who is in the other car?'

'I don't know.'

'Are we in trouble?'

'Not in broad daylight, no.' He opens the door. 'come on you lot, get your things.'

'Who's in the other car?'

'Terry, I don't know.'

'It's the feds.'

'In a limo? I doubt it.'

'I'll leave first', Mick hisses, sighing.

'Mick, they're here for all of us, whoever's in the other car. Let's all calm down, let's go and find out shall we?'

They open the main door and the stairs unwind. Mick goes ahead, then Terry and Jack. Adam and Sophia hold back, watching through the small tinted window to see who gets out of the other car.

'Adam, let's go, whoever it is they know we're on here.'

'Come on.'

They walk down the stairs holding hands, she a step behind him.

DC Williams gets out of the other limo with three undercover policemen, smirking at Adam. One handcuffs Jack, another tries to handcuff Adam.

'Whoa, you're not in uniform or on duty, you can't arrest me or him, let him go.' Now, uncuff him.' The officer does, knowing the limousine is paid for by Jerry and he could get into serious trouble being paid by him off duty. One of the other officers mimes, *'what the fuck?'*

'Oh really? Let me make a phone call,' says the officer. He dials airport security, screaming down the phone, 'Get the police, we have fugitives here at Bay Four, get them here immediately!'

'Get in the car, all of you!' screams Mick. 'Terry, get us out of here!'

All jump in and Terry speeds off as fast as he can, heading towards the barriers, with Dave dressed as the chauffeur in the front.

'Give me that pass, quick.' Dave hands Terry the pass and the guards check all the passports, looking quizzically at Terry with his head bent down.

'Go on.'

The barriers lift. Terry speeds off, hearing the sirens from the back of the airport and seeing the other car pulling up at the barrier with police cars in tow. 'Stall them, come on, stall them!' He looks in the rear mirror, seeing police approaching the limo at the barrier.

'Look Adam, Mick, would you look at that.'

'Focus, get us away, put your foot down and lose them, hurry up.'

'I'm on it aren't I bruv. Calm it, Mickey boy.'

'Where are we going?'

'A place they won't find us, Soph.' Terry smiles in the mirror.

'Like a safe house?'

'No, yes… no.' Adams taps his phone.

'Which?'

'Terry, take us into Kent, take a right here towards Brighton.'

'On it boss.'

'What's in Kent?'

'My other house, but it's in your name. They'll be all over London, your parents', my mother's.'

'Oh my gosh, we're fugitives on the run.'

'Not all of us, only Terry and Mick on a technicality.'

'Jack, are you okay?'

'Need my pain meds, left them in my rucksack on the floor.'

'Williams has them now.'

'At least he doesn't have my passport.'

'Jack, we'll stop at a pharmacy.'

'No we won't, take it like a man.'

'Mick he's kind of pale, he's sweating.'

'That's the morphine wearing off.'

'He needs more.'

'Enough, all of you. We get to the house, the driver will go and get some for him all right? You'll need to change Dave, take another car.'

'You're the boss, yes, I know just the place.'

'Are we nearly there?' Jack calls out in pain, wiping his fringe off his brow.

'Another ten minutes.' Adam types in the postcode, hands his phone to Terry. 'Follow that, come off at this junction.'

They pull into a country lane, speeding down the green winding road, Terry taking corners like he's on a Formula One racetrack. Sophia checks her watch: 5.30am Sunday morning. 'Thank you Jesus for getting us out of this mess' she says, sighing loudly.

'Hey, what's up?'

'Nothing, honestly I'm fine.'

'I know that look, tell me?'

'Beat it, yes, beat the nav didn't I, here we are.'

Electric gates unwind as Adam presses a black pad. In the centre of the driveway there's a fountain in the shape of an elegant naked man entwined with a woman. Tyres crunch over the gravel; a silver Mercedes and a black 4x4 Porsche sit beside a large yellow stone cottage with ivy growing up the sides of the windows, a red double door underneath arched brickwork.

'This is ours?' she whispers into his ear.

'It's yours, the Porsche is yours too.'

She blinks in disbelief, squeezing her hands together. Dave opens her door and helps her out and Adam climbs out behind her, takes her hand from Dave's, picks her up, presses the pad and the red doors open.

Terry, Mick and Jack sit in the car watching. 'Oi Dave, get in here, give them a few minutes.'

'I need my meds, man.'

Taking a set of keys from the glove compartment, Dave takes off his black tailored jacket, white shirt and tie.

'Oi, what are you doing bruv?'

'Looking casual, like he said.'

'Don't take anything else off.'

'Don't worry, I'm leaving my trousers and T-shirt on.'

'Thank fuck for that. You got money for the pharmacy?'

'Yes.'

'It isn't open yet for fuck's sake,' Mick hisses at Terry.

'Well he can find a 24-hour one can't he Mickey boy?'

'Terry, you're really getting on my wick, you know that? Being stuck with you on a yacht, a helicopter then a plane with your speeding, you're making me feel sick. Dave, how are you going to get morphine without a prescription?'

Terry looks at Mick, scratching the stubble on his face.

'Jack, you're just going to have to suffer. Let's go inside, see if there's anything to take the edge off. You did his shopping, Davy boy?'

'Everything is in the kitchen, straight through the lobby in the back. In the dining room there's a selection of bottles, plenty, so yes Terence, go, knock yourself out.'

'Come on Jack, let's get you a whisky.'

'No, fuck that, I want some vodka, neat and lots of it.'

CHAPTER 45

✦✦✦✦

The Comisaria de Policia walks up the stairs in his navy-blue suit; Nathan King hands over five thousand euros to the officer in reception for the release of his brother and nephew.

'No money, no, no.'

'Take it, I want them out. What have they done, what are they being charged for?'

'They are being released, no charge.'

'Would you tell me what the fuck is going on?'

'One minute, wait here.'

Nathan taps the money, slapping his black tattooed hand, his eye twitching. He looks down at his shiny brown leather shoes. Jet lagged, he walks over to the water fountain, fills a white plastic cup and drinks it, pressing the button for another. He smiles at his brother and nephew walking towards him, all hugging each other.

'Come on, I got a car outside, what the fuck is going on?'

'Dad wanted me to.'

'Enough.'

'No, you wanted to do another dirty fight, what have I told you about that?'

'Just drive us back to the villa.'

'I want an explanation. I had to get two fucking flights here.'

'Dad, are we safe going back to the villa, you know with the Colombians and that?'

'You're a stupid pair of idiots, I booked a hotel, we'll go there.'

'Yes, we're safe. Drive to the villa, it's Jerry they'll want, not us. We fucking got arrested, the Colombians won't touch us.'

'We're going to the hotel. If you two have hits on your heads and you're trying to do another rigged fight, then I am going to get shot, and no fucking way am I getting shot at in your villa. It's just here, Marbella Club Hotel – oi! Before we get out of this car, Matt, you done a rigged fight with that other fighter, why use your own son? I can't get my head around that. Go on, in a few words.'

'Because he's a knock-out champion, he got balls. He could have done it, nobody would have suspected anything, it's a boxing match, people get killed.'

'He's your own fucking son, have you completely

lost it? And how did it get ambushed, why were you two arrested?

'Someone snitched.'

'You have to ask yourself who. Have you done that? Who do you think snitched and where are they?'

'We don't know do we, been locked up all night, questioned.'

'What questions?'

'Ah man, you know the drill.'

'I haven't been arrested Matt, no, so spit it out, I want to know why it got hit by the feds, why you two, what did they say?'

'Said they got a tip off I was going to kill Wright, someone bugged dad.'

'And you didn't check, you idiot? Let's drive to the airport, get out of this place, what do you reckon?'

'Where?'

'The next available place on the screens, I don't know, just away from here. You two stay here, I'll get your passports. Don't bother about your clothes, you can buy some where we're going.'

Junior's in the back checking his Blackberry for flights, biting his cut bottom lip. He's paranoid they are going to get shot at. He looks at the sign of the hotel, knowing the Kellys own it.

'Majorca is the next, three seats left. Here look dad, leaves in three hours.'

'Book it J, book the seats, we're getting out of here, it

stinks. You two, the room key is here, get out. I'll come back for you.'

'I'm not getting out, I want to stay with you.'

'Get out son!'

'Dad, you do know who owns this hotel?'

'Fuck, we're staying together.'

Danny is on the balcony, making calls with the baby underneath an umbrella in her pushchair. Alena is dressed in tight short denims, white flats, and a white chemise showing her bra. She has a high ponytail with a black velvet hair tie and she is packing two Louis Vuitton brown cases. She gets the baby's clothes, neatly folds them off the airier, then puts them into a pink rucksack, followed by a pack of nappies, baby wipes, boiling water. She makes eight bottles up, four of milk and four for water for their journey back home.

'You going to shower? I put your shorts out, wear these black ones.'

'No, get me other ones out.'

'Ah, I just packed, wear these.'

'Unpack, I want the other ones.'

'Which?'

'The light blue ones, polo.'

'And your T-shirt?'

'Fuck knows, whatever goes with me shorts.'

'Fuck you.'

'Fuck you too bitch, come here.' He gets out of his

chair and walks over to her, then pulls the bedclothes off the bed and throws her down, kissing her and staring into her blue eyes. He twists her ponytail around her face, strokes her chin, holds her neck at the back, pulling her head back and kissing and licking her collarbone.

'You fucking sexy bitch, you ready for me?' He undoes her shorts and pulls them off, wraps her white G-string in his thumb and forefinger and tears it off, hearing the ripping sound.

Alena gasps, 'huh, ah… Danny…'

'Yes?'

'Danny, yes.'

The two hitmen sigh as they listen to the Irish gangster talking dirty into his pretty tanned wife's ear. They're waiting for them to hurry up and leave.

Nathan pulls over at a busy breakfast bar, the Blue Palm, filled with holidaymakers. 'You two get something to eat, I'll go and get your things, where are they?'

'In the safe, as per.'

'What's the code?'

'54321.'

'Who chose that?'

'I'm not getting out of this car in these shorts. Just take us back, nobody's going to do anything.'

'Glad you're the lucid one now. Half an hour ago you were a right paranoid idiot.'

'Nathan, he's right, it's not our heads they want, it's the two Irish families. They're at war, we just...'

'Got caught up with them, I get it. Right, I am going in there ordering some food, what you want?'

'Full English.'

'No son, your diet.'

'Dad, fuck my diet, a full English.'

'All right son, keep your knickers on, yeah get me one, too will you?'

They're sitting in the car parked outside, all eating in silence, scoffing salmon and scrambled eggs, drinking a bottle of cold water, passing over paper napkins. Matt and Junior are digging into their breakfast with plastic knives and forks. They down the bottles of water, put the trash in a bag. Nathan gets out and puts it all on an empty table. He opens the car door, gets in and looks at Junior in the mirror.

'You all right?'

'Yeah, ate too fast... can't breathe.'

'He's fucking choking.'

'Do something, Matt.'

'Get out son.' Matt opens his door, pulling him out, holding him up. Nathan gets out his side and runs around, seeing his brother do a Heimlich manoeuvre. Junior spits his food out and starts being sick at the kerb. Everyone's watching, holding their mouths. Someone shouts, 'That's him, the boxer, King you all right?'

'Yeah he is, get in the car son.'

A pretty brunette, long wavy curls, big brown eyes, tanned skin, white knee-length linen dress, walks over with some tissues and a big bottle of water and passes them to him. 'Good fight, it's on us, here.'

'Thank you.' Staring eyes lock on as Nathan winds up the windows and drives off, heading to the villa.

'Pretty wasn't she?'

'Yeah, go back get her number for me.'

'On our way back later J.'

'What if she isn't there? Turn around, now.'

CHAPTER 46

✦✦✦✦

'What are we going to do?' Jack tries to stretch forward.

'Don't know, we can't do anything until those two come downstairs. Try and get some sleep.'

'I was asleep all day yesterday. No, I want to do something. I'm bored just sitting here.'

'Have another drink then.'

'Pass it over.'

'Here.'

Mick is fast asleep on the corner sofa on the other side of the large living room. Terry is sitting on the armchair opposite Jack's, doing neck stretches, rolling his head around. They pass the bottle of Absolut vodka to each other.

'It's finished.'

'Well, get another, there's plenty. Knock yourself out,

you soon will anyway if you drink like a fish.'

'It's numbing the pain.'

'See, told you didn't I?'

'I can't sit back properly, it hurts like hell.'

'First time it always does.'

'How many times have you been shot?'

'Three.'

'Three! And you're laughing?'

'Can't cry over spilt milk can you?'

'Where?'

'One here, look at that scar. Went straight through the leg.'

'Who shot you?'

'Can't tell you that.'

'Where else?'

Terry stands up, pulling up his orange T-shirt.

'One here, almost killed me this one, had to have surgery. This one fucking hurt, the others weren't a patch on this fucker here.'

'Whoa man!'

'Here as well, right on the back of my shoulder, but a bit higher than yours, that's why I thought you'd be okay. I didn't think it had punctured your lung and I studied anatomy.'

'Bollocks you did. Shut the fuck up, you're getting louder.'

'Oh, sorry Mickey boy, we're drinking to our war wounds.'

'They awake yet?'

'Didn't know they were asleep. Probably they're… you know.'

'Well, we're not, she is, I had an hour, we have business to do.'

'No, these two are drunk, not fit for anything.'

'I heard on my way down, how much have you had?'

'Only this bottle, he needs it to…'

'I get it. Where's Dave?'

'Isn't back yet.'

'Jack, listen, I'm driving you to the police station.'

'What for?'

'This.'

Adam plays him the audio. Jack listens to himself, eyes widening, looking at Adam, biting his lips together nervously, listening.

'What about it? You set me up, recording me.'

'I'm being framed for murdering his wife.'

'Whoa man, I know.'

'Jerry's. That blue jumper he took out of the Jag, it's mine.'

'What was it doing in his car?'

'Jack, he took it off my chair, we were in a restaurant and I forgot about it. Now can we go?'

'Wait, so you arranged the whole thing to save me, to save you?'

'Eh… yes.'

'You got me shot?'

'Don't be stupid.'

'Don't call me stupid, I have to think. You kidnapped me to get you off for murder, how do I know you didn't do it?'

'Use your nut!' Mick shouts across the room. He gets up and walks over to them.

'We were in a police chase Jack, you would be dead by now. That officer works for Jerry, they go way back. Adam didn't kill anyone. All of us did this for you, now show some fucking respect and come with us.'

'What about my meds?'

'The station doctor will give you some. Now please, we have to go to the local station, you have to tell them everything. I'll probably be arrested, I wasn't allowed to leave the country. It's down to you. You'll be interrogated, and I'll be in there for more than 24 hours if you don't tell them everything. Gary's on his way here.'

'Who's Gary?'

'Your barrister, he'll look out for you.'

'Fine, you did save my life. Twice.'

'See kid, now you're getting it.' Terry winks at him.

Adam scratches his head and walks out of the room, dialling Dave on the phone.

'Where are you, how long? Fine.'

'Your meds will be here in two minutes, now drink water and plenty of it, you need to sober up. You can't mix alcohol with morphine, and I need you alive.'

CHAPTER 47

✦✦✦✦

They are walking out of the airport. Nathan is wearing a pair of Matt's cream shorts, a grey T-shirt, grey Armani sandals, while Matt sports a pair of blue denim shorts, white polo shirt, white Gucci flipflops and Junior is in black shorts, grey string vest, black Gucci sandals. They climb into a white Mercedes cab.

'Take us to St Regis Hotel Resort please.'

'Nice one Nathan, been here before, nice touch.'

'Romantic. You going to ring her, send her a ticket? Matt and I are going to a meeting.'

'Who with?'

'Jerry, getting your money.'

'Is he here? Word is he's in London.'

'If he doesn't turn up will he wire it?'

'Oh, he will be here, he owes us son.'

'Yeah. Shall I ring her?'

'You loved up at first sight?'

'That chick is hot, yes, ring her.'

'What if she says no?'

'The way she looked at you son, I doubt it.'

'She couldn't keep her eyes off you.'

'Yeah but...'

'She wrote her number down, so ring her, get her on the next flight.'

'What if she blows me off?'

'Listen son, don't doubt yourself, I keep telling you.'

'Make the call.'

'Ah you two, just shut it, I'll ring her later.'

'I know that face. Slow down, oi, driver! Pull over, stop the car.'

Matt gets out and walks across the dual carriageway towards Danny and his wife pushing the baby stroller.

'Danny, it's me, how you doing?'

'All right, and you?'

'Sorry, heard the news, really sorry. My condolences to you and the family.'

'Ah, thanks Matt. What are you doing here? Thought you'd be back to the USA by now, after the fight.'

'We're taking a break, been locked in a cell all night. What are you guys doing here?'

'Been on holiday, checked our bags in an hour ago to miss the queue. We're just having a wee walk, getting some lunch, want to join us?'

'No, we're off to a meeting with Jerry.'

'Word is he won't leave London, you sure he's here, where?'

'Better be. Whoa, who's that, what the…?'

Nathan and Junior are sitting in the car on the other side of the dual carriageway, sighing and tutting at the time Matt is taking.

'He can talk.'

'He's a businessman, must be sorting something out.'

'Yeah, who are they?'

'Don't know, I recognise the face though. She's got a tight arse, fit as fuck isn't she?'

'No, too skinny. I like mine with meat on, something to grab on to if you get me.'

Gunshots. Junior is shouting. 'What the fuck, my dad, no, no, fuck!'

He's seeing Matt and Danny on the floor, Alena screaming, bending down.

'Someone call an ambulance! Danny, oh baby, what have they done, look at me Danny, look at me please, wake up, don't die, baby no, no…'

While the driver calls for an ambulance, Nathan and Junior run across the road. Junior lifts Matt's head.

'Matt, the ambulance is on the way,' says Nathan. Alena's screaming into Danny's chest as he breathes his last breath.

'Junior, get in the taxi, meet us at the hospital. Who was that, did you see them, Junior?'

'Oh my god, is he going to die?'

'Junior, get away from here! If they come back they'll shoot you too. Get in the taxi, get to the hospital, now.'

Ambulances pull over, sirens blaring, the police behind. An officer takes the stroller, another one pulls Alena off Danny's body, holding her.

'Get off me! Give me my baby, now!'

Nathan stands, letting the paramedics perform CPR on Danny, to no avail. The police are marking around Danny's body with yellow chalk. The paramedics are just looking down at him, shaking their heads. People gather around and across the road. Junior is sitting crying in the back of the taxi, the ambulance blocking his view of his dad.

CHAPTER 48

✦✦✦✦

Adam makes several calls, sends Detective Sergeant Thomas evidence and Jack's audio proving he was with Jerry and sent to Marbella, instead of turning up for his new role at Mitro Advertising Ltd.

Gary follows Jack into Surrey Police Station. The officers await the crucial arrival. One of them opens the locked brown door, wondering who the guy is that Jack has in tow.

Adam walks inside and greets Detective Sergeant Thomas.

'Phew, you got yourself into a right mess. Come on in, we'll look into every element at this stage with the evidence you gave me.'

Adam walks into a room and sits on a blue chair. There are files on the desk. He shows DS Thomas the photographs of Jerry and Matt on the yacht. Then he plays the audio again on the phone. Adam and Thomas look awkward as they listen to Matt King describing the killing of Kim Wright, in the MGM minutes before the boxing fight:

'Jerry wants you to kill him, the cartels and Colombians too, Jerry is paying you a lot of money for this...'

Beeping sounds on the breast pocket police radio speaker. DS Thomas turns the sound up and listens with concentration.

'Matt King and Danny O'Connor have been murdered in Majorca, pronounced dead at the scene,' says Thomas. 'Wait here.' He leaves the room, closes the door and walks down to the interview room, scratching his head as he listens in to Jack's interrogation about being offered a promotion from Sophia and Jerry agreeing to his new role in the advertising company; firing Sophia in front of Jack on the same day he got promoted for his new role, then Sophia re-hired. Why did Jerry fire and re-hire her a week before he was offered a million-dollar contract in Marbella?

He opens the brown door and sits reading Jack's statement. He listens to Jack rambling incoherently about the facts but brings things up to date about Jerry's sickening acts and that he was being trained to fight too, oblivious that he was being trained to be killed.

'You mentioned earlier that you got in his car. Focus on that, what happened?'

'You have the audio.'

'Tell them, you're on camera, they need the facts from you, the audio isn't enough.'

'Gary, I can't remember.'

'Can I have a word with my client?'

'Interview terminated at 11.40am, you have five minutes.'

'Pull it together Jack, start by leaving the pub, remember?'

'Right.'

Gary opens the door. 'He's ready, needs more water. Can you prove who shot Jack?'

'Not yet, we're working with the Spanish detectives. Interview commences 11.43. Jack, continue?'

'I was walking out of the pub, staggering down the street, and Jerry pulled over offering me a ride home. I got in, we drove around the corner and he pulled over, took a blue sweater and asked me to wait, so I did.'

'What time was that?'

'I don't know, almost dark.'

'How long were you waiting for?'

'About ten minutes.'

'How was Jerry when he got back to his car?'

'Fine, asked if I wanted a drink in a pub. Look, it's all on the audio man.'

'We have all we need for now Jack, you're free to go. We'll be in touch.'

'Wait – what about protecting my client from...?'

'Gary, we cannot offer him police protection at this stage.'

'Why not? Without it, he might die before the trial.'

'We'll see what we can do. I'll call you later, update you, look after him.'

'I am not his babysitter.'

'No, but Adam seems to have got him out of that idiot's hands. Make sure he stays out of trouble.'

Detective Sergeant Thomas nods, concluding that Jack was the missing piece of the jigsaw. That confirms they have enough evidence that Jerry was guilty of murdering his wife with extreme violence, with no respect for humanity whatsoever. But he wants more evidence of money laundering as well...

Thomas walks back inside and nods over at Adam, indicating for him to leave the room.

'Go home, get some sleep, you look like shit. I'll handle it from here. The audios have been sent around to everyone I know. Make sure you lock him up and throw away the key, Jack will be safe with me. Really we should lock you up for leaving the country.'

'I had to, otherwise it would be me inside for life. I got Jack out of trouble and handed him to you on a silver platter.'

'Smart arse. I'll call you later.'

CHAPTER 49

✦✦✦✦

Priggish Andrew Kelly in white shorts, a white shirt, unbuttoned, showing his grey hairy chest, a heavy fat stomach, tanned skin, grey short hair with big blue eyes, is keeping a low profile. He is sitting on a black leather recliner chair in his six-million-euro villa south of Marbella, rubbing his hands together with glee as he studies his Apple Mac. He moves his head from side to side, forefinger on the mouse to click on the purchase of a cargo container ship from Somalia to import more illicit contraband.

He is wiring illegitimate money into Jerry's account following the deaths of the O'Connor brothers. He wants him to take action on the rest of the family, so he is sending him only half the three million pounds because he has not yet killed Kim Wright. He bites his lips together, hissing at himself, knowing he has to pay the Colombians their money back. As he ponders how to strike a deal, he rubs his lips with his forefinger and thumb and wipes the saliva from his mouth, tapping his temple as he conjures up a plan in his head. He rubs his hands together again, thinking how to not pay back 15 million dollars or the hit will be on his head. Buy the cargo ship, offer to pick up 300 kilograms of cocaine in Peru, sign port concession contract on the north coast – that should do it.'

Andrew is dealing with the wholesale distribution of food across to Ireland in shipping containers, opening shops in Dublin, smuggling drugs but protecting himself, keeping his hands clean. Twenty-four men are working for him distributing cannabis and cocaine worldwide. But he's pissed off, unable to get his head around his brother Gordon being shot dead right outside the Regis last year on the orders of Kenny O'Connor. He will have revenge at all costs. He is keeping Raymond and Ivan in Ireland, running the industrial estate and shops back in Dublin. He doesn't want his younger brothers caught up in the crossfire. He wants to keep his family safe, his ex-wife and five children. Andrew is protected wherever he travels around Marbella and Malaga.

Interpol is working with Scotland Yard, the Spanish undercover agents working together to take down the international crime gang. Andrew is untouchable, never leaving his villa, always using old Nokia phones with different sim cards. Jerry, on the other hand, is not so smart. He uses his office phone to liaise with DC Williams, not mentioning anything other than the update of Adam's trial due this month, but he is completely unaware that Williams' phone is bugged, along with his car, two belts and three pairs of shoes, all bugged in his tiny one-bedroom flat in East London. Jerry's car and his central London apartment are also bugged. Agents have taken down the spotlights and fitted bugs before twisting them back in place. They have also bugged four tailored Savile Row suit collars.

Scotland Yard wanted more evidence that Jerry is taking illicit money. They want to arrest him for the murder of his wife, but first they are searching for everything they can pin on him, biding their time, intent on proving without shadow of a doubt the positive outcome of this operation. They know now that with Jack, the last piece of the puzzle, they have enough evidence to put him away.

CHAPTER 50

✦✦✦✦

Two gold-plated caskets lie in Mrs O'Connor's large living room, flowers abundant on different tables and stands, Debussy playing quietly in the background. All the immediate family and two priests are inside, everyone dressed in black. Outside, friends of this well-known family are gathering, and they too are all dressed in black.

Adam has opted for a dark grey silk suit with a black shirt and tie. Jack is in a black suit borrowed from Terry, who wears a white shirt and black tie. Mick is in a navy-blue tailor-made suit with a blue handkerchief in the breast pocket and a blue silk shirt. Sophia is wearing a knee-length black dress, black flat shoes, a black Canada goose poncho and black sunglasses, and holding Maria's hand. Maria is wearing a flowing black ankle-length dress with a black jacket, high-heeled black Jimmy Choos and tinted silver sunglasses. She is weeping into a tissue.

Two black hearses pull up outside the house, watched by uninvited people who are filling the street to pay their respects. Six O'Connor brothers carry Kenny's coffin into one hearse, while six cousins carry Danny's. Chrysanthemums form Kenny's and Danny's names in the windows on the hearses. The drivers slowly pull away, people lining the street crying, watching the family all holding onto one another behind the cars on the short walk to the familiar St Patrick's Cathedral. Mick holds Maria's hand, seeing how unsteadily she walks on the cobbled road. I got you, come on now it's not that far,' he says.

'I want to see him. Will they open it inside like we do in Spain?'

'I don't know.'

'I hope, because I want to kiss him goodbye.'

'I'm pretty sure they do,' interjects Adam. 'it's how they do this over here Maria, it's tradition, and the service will go on for two hours in there. We'll have to sit at the back.'

'Why?'

'In case the Kellys come.'

'They wouldn't, not in a sacred place of worship?' Sophia whispers to Adam.

'It's been known. You two are sitting in the far back corner. If the other family do decide to come, they will go straight for the family in the front, so I want you two out of the way.'

'Adam you're scaring us! Shush with this nonsense, nobody will come and shoot at a funeral.'

'Sophia, it's been done before, the Irish are well known for attacking funerals.'

Sophia gasps, holding her breath. Maria takes off her glasses and looks at Sophia's face, pale with horror. Sophia bows her head down and bites her lip, whispering to Adam, 'why not just shoot them on the walk?'

'It's how they deliver their message. It's a gang war, they have no care whatsoever for humanity, they're evil.'

'I'm not going inside, I'll wait outside, sit on a bench. He was your friend, not mine.'

'As you wish.'

At last the gilded caskets are carried out of the cathedral by the brothers and cousins. The family come out behind, all walking out towards the graveside, followed by everybody else.

Adam walks over to the bench, grasps Sophia's hand. 'Come on.'

'See, I told you nothing would happen.'

'Still might yet, over there at the plots.'

'Adam, enough, please!'

'I know this isn't the time or place, but I'm in danger as well as Jack and the other brothers'

'Oh I am sorry, I forgot, I just thought that at a funeral it would be ok and go smoothly. Are Mick and Terry armed?'

'Of course they are.'

'But if they use a sniper, how they are going to protect us all?'

'Mick and Terry are walking around, checking for cars, you can guess the rest.'

All gather around the two plots, side by side; the brothers and cousins lower the coffins into the ground and everyone sobs into their tissues, holding hands, putting arms around each other, hearing the priest.

'Forasmuch as it hath pleased Almighty God of his great mercy to take unto himself the soul of our dear brothers here departed, we therefore commit their bodies to the ground; earth to earth, ashes to ashes, dust to dust; in sure and certain hope of the Resurrection to eternal life, through our Lord Jesus Christ, Amen.'

CHAPTER 51

✦✦✦✦

Jerry, livid about the amount in his account, is dialling Andrew's phone, but the line is dead. He tries another number, and that doesn't work either. Then he dials DC Williams from his office phone.

'We got a problem, you on duty?'

'No, start back Sunday. No news on where they are still, why, what's up?'

'Come to the office.'

'No, I'll stick out too much, I'm in jeans.'

'It's dress down Friday here, everyone's casual, you'll blend right in.'

'What's up, just tell me?'

'You have to come to my office, too risky being seen together.'

'On my way.'

Jerry picks up the phone and dials Elaine. 'Oi, get me some Chinese and plenty of drinks.'

'What kind of drinks?'

'You know what I want, get on it now.'

'I'm on it, Jerry.'

'Good, hurry up.'

He picks up the phone and dials Elaine again.

'Go out and get me a bottle of bourbon and a bag of ice.'

'Right away.'

He hangs up and looks at his reflection in the cabinet window, standing tall, chest puffed out in his brown tailor-made suit, smiling smugly at his dominant figure and his big veneers. He laughs, mutters to himself. He is looking forward to the trial next Tuesday. He's untouchable here in London. *Fuck Andrew, the cartel will see to him all right and I'm as free as a fucking bird. He can screw the rest of the fucking millions he owes me, I got plenty you fucking scumbag, you're finished anyway.*

Williams walks in on him, sees his lips move through the glass pane.

'Who are you talking to?'

'Just having a ramble, we got a problem.'

'You have, you mean.'

Elaine knocks on the door. 'Bring it in then, leave it on the desk, off you trot.'

She closes the door and they watch her walk towards

the elevator, waiting for clearance, sees the silver elevator door slide shut.

'Drink?'

'Oh, I'm going to need it I reckon, glasses?'

'In the cabinet, get the glasses, I'll get the ice. Hungry?'

'No, I just ate. What's up?'

'How come you can't find them when they were in Ireland yesterday?'

'I've been away with the Mrs, what you got?'

'They're living in a cottage in Surrey, that's what I got. I want you to get Jack.'

'I'm not signed up for this, almost cost me my job last week at the airport, had to come up with a right bullshit story. Plus you're not paying me enough, why can't your guys get him?'

'Jack has to go.'

'Yeah I know, we have three days to figure it out.'

'I need it sorting, otherwise I am done. Get him. How much more money do you want?'

'Half of what Andrew Kelly paid you.'

Jerry spits out an ice cube,

'You what?'

'You heard.'

'My men are watching the cottage, trying to get a shot, the others are armed inside, fucking gay fuckwits.'

'Who's gay?'

'The fucking black bastard I invited on the yacht next to mine. It's Adam's hitmen, watching me for a week. I get it now, but they got fuck all on me. They aren't gay, they were fucking acting, the slimy twats. You need to get Jack arrested, can you do that?'

'You are paying me?'

'Of course, but Andrew only transferred half, see for yourself, it's on the account there. I can't pay you that amount, what about a quarter of a mill?'

'Half.'

'No can do I'm afraid.'

'Then our business is done. If they can't get a shot at Jack, I can't get involved any more, it's out of my hands. I'm leaving.'

'Wait, okay, half a million, if you can get a warrant and get him arrested.'

'Jerry, I can, but you're not thinking straight.'

'Go on?'

'Look, I don't want any more money now.'

'You having a wobble on me now?'

'If I get a warrant, get him arrested, you want me to kill him in the cell?'

'Now you're talking my language.'

'Jerry, it's impossible.'

'Why?'

'They all have CCTV in the cells now, live streaming all the time.'

'Slip something in his drink then.'

'I'll do it Sunday when I'm on duty, say I got a lead. What's the address?'

'Shortwood Common, Staines TW18.'

'You're transferring the money now?'

CHAPTER 52

✦✦✦✦

In the all-white master bedroom, I tread softly on the fluffy carpet, not wanting to wake him. I open the bathroom door, close it behind me. I hold my stomach and look into my reflection in the mirror, then wipe my eyes with my fingers. Then I sit on the pouffe in the corner, counting in my head how many days since my last period, biting my lip. I'm late. I don't want to tell him, not with all the work going on. How long is she staying for, how long are they all here for, when will it all be over?

Slowly opening the door, I pick up my cream jumper and slip on my jeans, watching him fast asleep. I open the door quietly and shut it softly after me. Then I walk past three closed white doors, Jack in one bedroom, Maria in another and Terry…

Terry opens his door, startled. 'Huh, morning.'

'Shh, anyone else awake?'

'No, not sure if anyone is downstairs. Dave and Mick are still down there on watch. Yeah I'll go, so one of them can get some shuteye.'

'I'll put the kettle on, what time is it?'

'Five thirty-five. Yeah, I would love a cuppa.'

I hear the birds sing and look out the window, trying to see them in the oaks outside as dawn breaks in the one-acre back garden. I turn around to the sound of the silver kettle whistling. I take an oven glove and hold the black rubber handle, placing it on the wooden sideboard, then stretch my arms in the air in a star shape.

Arms around my tummy, hugging me from behind – Adam. He closes my arms around his, pulls my head into his chest.

'I was awake, why didn't you kiss me good morning?'

'You were snoring, you fibber.'

'Not watching you get dressed I wasn't.'

'Sneaky.'

'How long were you in the bathroom? I mean, you didn't use the toilet or sink.'

'Why are you spying on me?'

'I heard you mumbling something to yourself, what is it?'

I pour the contents of the kettle into a large cafetière, smelling the aroma of the ground caffeine, concentrating. I take a wooden spoon and stir the coffee before turning around to face him. I kiss his lips softly.

'Good morning.'

'Good morning yourself. What did you say?'

'Adam, it's nothing really, coffee?'

'Yes please. How late are you?'

I roll my tongue around the inside of my mouth.

'Stop doing that, you always do that when you overthink. How late?'

'Two weeks, I think.'

'We'll do a test.'

'Adam, it's too early.'

'Is it?'

'How long is she staying for, how long is this going to go on for?'

'Word is a couple more days I'm afraid.'

'Just feels kind of weird being stuck inside all the time.'

'It's for your safety, Jack's mainly, but you can go out, with Mick Dave or Terry. I'll go out later and get the test, what are they called?'

'No, let's wait.'

'Sophia, really?'

'A few more weeks?'

'Why?'

'Do you, are you, do you…'

'Yes, more than anything, wedding plans, mother will arrange all of it.'

'Let's wait.'

'Why?'

'It's all too fast.'

'Babe, I love you, this is the best news ever, why aren't you happy?'

'Adam, if you really want us to do the test, we will, but we can't tell a single soul. It's got to be kept a secret. We have to keep our mouths closed until we're over the twelve-week stage.'

'Why, will you be showing by then?'

'I don't know, why?'

'Because mother will arrange the wedding. I won't tell anyone we're having a baby, but I'll tell her to start the plans when I come back from Marbella tomorrow.'

'What? Why are you going back over there?'

'It's my job.'

'But everyone is here.'

'James is my client, I have to take Maria back as well.'

'Who is James?'

'You met him last week in Ireland at the wake, remember – James O'Connor.'

'What about us here?'

'Maria and I are on the six o' clock plane later this evening, it's booked.'

'Uh, seriously? It's dangerous over there, I don't like your work.'

'James is with his seven brothers sorting out their business and he pays me, I have to be there.'

'Why can't you do it on the phone?'

'It doesn't work like that.'

'Why not?'

'Just doesn't.'

'Adam you're a barrister here, not in Spain.'

'Babe, I am fluent in Spanish, we have a company over there.'

'You do?'

'Why do you think I have to represent my clients over there?'

'You never mentioned this before, what else do you have up your sleeve?'

'You know I don't discuss work.'

'Adam, you are something else.'

I stand in the corner, leaning on the side worktop, a hand on my hip. I lower my elbow and rest my head on it, looking over at him sighing. He's sitting opposite me on a high white stool, glaring at me, smiling.

Terry walks in.

'Parched here, any coffee left? What's up with you two? I kind of heard you were in a deep conversation about going back over tonight. What about me, am I coming? Love that place.'

'No, you're staying here.'

'Ah bruv.' Making two mugs of coffee walking back out onto the marble floor, pale yellow decor, dining area back into the living room, closing the door handing Dave a coffee. 'Oi Mickey, get some rest for a couple hours, there's a good boy.'

Mick yawns and gets off the corner sofa, peeps out of the vertical blinds, gets up, walks out of the room, goes upstairs into his bedroom, passing Jack on the way up.

'Stay away from the windows, that's an order.'

'Good morning to you too! Yeah, I know, stay out of the way, you going to sleep?'

'Yes, Dave and Terence are down there.'

'Okay.' Jack wipes his eyes and sits on the bottom stair, yawning.

'Breakfast, Soph?'

'Hmm, sounds good, what shall we have?'

'What do we have babe? You sit here, I'm cooking.'

'The fridge is full. You're cooking?'

'For you, yes.' I scratch my temple and walk over to the high white table. I sit on the stool with a mug of coffee, hands wrapped around the china, watching him take out eggs, bacon, beans, tomatoes, basil, honey, pancake mix, milk. He walks over to me and puts a dried peach in my mouth.

'Full English, pancakes, what would you like?'

'Wow, all of it!'

Adam walks back over to the side cupboard, taking out pans and pots. Jack walks in. 'Morning what's for breakfast?'

'Jack, get out of here now.'

Jack goes out, shutting the white double doors, and three gunshots pierce three holes in the white double doors. Adam freezes. Sophia is on the floor, bending down, Adam crawling over to her.

CHAPTER 53

✦✦✦✦

Four black Range Rovers pull onto the pavement; armed police enter the office doors. Jerry is tucking into his crispy duck with hoisin sauce, shredded spring onions and cucumber, rolling his pancakes, watching Williams leave in the elevator, smiling at his food. He's oblivious, not watching the screens, eating as fast as he can, swigging his drink, eating another one really fast, biting and chewing with a nasty crunching sound of bone.

Finally he looks at the screens.

'You fucker.'

He spits a veneer out on to the desk. Looking up now at the screens, his eyes are widening, knowing he's going to be arrested, nowhere to flee.

'They got fuck all on me,' he's muttering.

In reception, he can see two officers pointing their

guns into Williams' face. He shuts down the two laptops and runs around the desk, trying to slide them underneath the cabinet. He looks out of the window and sees the four blacked-out cars. The silver elevator door opens and four armed officers with guns burst into his office. One officer shouts 'Arms in the air, now', another cuffs him.

'You're under arrest on suspicion of the murder of Lucy Cunningham, conspiring to kill Kim Wright in Marbella, the murders of two other men, and money laundering. You have the right to remain silent. Anything you do say may be used in evidence against you before the court, do you understand?'

'Yes.'

DC Williams is sitting in one of the cars, handcuffed, shaking his head; he looks out of the window and sees everybody in the office windows up above looking down at him. He watches, sees Jerry handcuffed, his head being bent forward as he is shepherded into the back of another Range Rover. From the windows of the other offices, faces peer out, smearing off condensation to get a clearer view.

One armed officer takes out plastic bags. 'Nutter, that was fucking great hearing all of that, least we got evidence now. Here, put these gloves on. You get his mobile, I'll get the two laptops, let's scour the place for anything else.'

'You think we got enough evidence, recording him and that?'

'Look kid, I know you're new to this. We just heard

he got paid off the Kelly cartel in Marbella – you did hear him, didn't you?'

'Yes, but he didn't admit to anything, did he.'

'He's just transferred money into an officer's account for the hit on Jack.'

'Who is Jack?'

'Where the fuck were you on Monday and Tuesday's briefing on this case? You were there!'

'Oh, I get it, that's the one he wants killed, he's the witness.'

'Finally! Here, put this laptop in this bag, that one in the other. Why are your hands shaking?'

'Told you, it's adrenaline. Sorry sir, it's my first day, I'm too pumped up, I didn't expect it to happen as quick as it did.'

'How long did you train for?'

'Six months, finished eight months ago.'

'No wonder. The first time is always a shocker, we never know if shooters are going to be aimed at us.'

'Yeah, that's what I was kind of expecting.'

'It's what we're trained for, but six months ago?'

'Yeah, had to do two months of theory.'

'You're supposed to do that before the assault training.'

'I did.'

'How come this is your first?'

'I got a lucky break, got a free holiday. Went to Majorca, I was there at the scene when Danny O'Connor got shot, fucking horrible.'

'And that was your first dead body scenario?'

'No, did a stint on the motorways. I asked for this, it's what I am trained for, not the highway stuff.'

'You'll be fine, let's wrap this up, get out of here.'

'What about the office, that Elaine woman?'

'Kid, officers are on it, use your nut.'

CHAPTER 54

✦✦✦✦

Dave and Terry run out the front doors; Mick's firing his rifle from the bedroom window into the trees at the back. Terry hears an exhaust and shouts to Dave, 'Get in, tail them, I'll take this car, you take that, hurry up Dave.'

Driving around the country lanes, they try to pass the Friday rush hour commuters. Terry sees up ahead a black tinted Mercedes and drives on the pavement to get closer; Dave follows him. The lights turn to red, the black car speeds off and Terry brakes, almost hitting a woman with a stroller on the corner. Dave brakes hard but can't avoid hitting Terry. People are sitting on their phones in their cars at the lights. Terry and Dave speed off, but in seconds they're behind more cars on a single-carriageway road. The Merc is out of sight, and they're still flashing the headlights for other drivers to pull over. Dave dials, 'take the motorway.'

'They've gone, turn around we're going back to the house, give it up Terry.'

'Fuck, right, fuck!'

'I know, come on, they've gone mate.'

Adam's holding onto Sophia, checking for bullet wounds on her body. He picks her up off the floor, checking for marks.

'Adam, I'm fine, I just jumped onto the floor.'

'You're shaking, you're in shock babe, the baby?'

Terry and Dave screech to a halt outside, Terry runs upstairs. 'They've gone, we lost them, fucking cops will be on the way now. Mick, stop shooting.'

Ambulances and police cars pull into the gates; Terry opens the door, letting them inside. 'Everyone's fine, but come in anyway.'

Sophia is being treated for shock; the paramedics are giving her water and sugar in a plastic cup. The police take Jack into a lounge on the right through the dining area, asking Maria to leave the room. They start questioning Adam. In reception police are taking statements from Dave, Maria and Jack. Terry is being handcuffed. 'You're under arrest on suspicion of dangerous driving. You have the right to remain silent, but anything you do say will be used in evidence, do you understand?'

'They're fucking arresting us!' he screams. He is led out to a police car.

Dave is also being arrested and handcuffed. Adam walks out, hearing Terry's protest. 'Sergeant Thomas, can you please uncuff them?' he says. 'They are trained ex-police, we need them to ensure Jack, our witness isn't killed – please?'

Thomas frowns and lets out a sigh.

'You're really trying my patience, Adam. Fine, we'll mark up the scene, try and get photo footage of the black Mercedes. They have to be charged with the offences, I'm afraid.'

'You're losing sight of all of this. They are protecting us, and you lot haven't got any guns. My fiancée is pregnant, and I'm concerned that this whole experience with you lot here will...'

'Uncuff them.'

'Sir? What?'

'You heard, uncuff them now.'

'Thank you so much.'

'You owe me, and Adam, we're on the case, listening into Jerry and DC Williams, been listening now for a couple of days.'

'And?'

'Nothing yet.'

'Shit.'

'You're on trial Tuesday, this is fucked up.'

'Tell me about it.'

'We'll mark up the ranges from outside, we're going to be a while. You know how it works, take the girls out if you don't want them to be around all the carnage.'

'I owe you.'

'Bet your life you do.'

Maria's arm is around Sophia, holding her hand in the quiet lounge, sitting on a two-seater brown sofa, a brown coffee table in front of their feet. The vertical blinds are closed, and three spotlights shine above their heads.

'This is crazy Sophia.'

'Tell me about it, at least Jack is okay.'

'And you?'

'You want another drink?'

'No, I'm fine. You're leaving with Adam tonight, he's booked your flights.'

'What time?'

'Six.'

'I don't want to, I'll stay for you, if you'd like me to?'

'Honestly, I'm driving up to my parent's house this evening, Adam has work to do and you must go back. James has taken over MGM. Dave, Mick and Terry will keep Jack safe here.'

CHAPTER 55

✦✦✦✦

Sophia's upstairs on her Mac drawing up a contract, sipping green tea with the smart TV on and listening to YouTube, which blocks out all the commotion downstairs. Adam walks in with a plate of fruit and a jug of water.

'Hey you.'

'Hey yourself. What do you think about this?'

'Let's have a look.' He studies her work. 'You missed something.'

'Where?'

'I'm leaving him in charge of all my work if I go down after the trial.'

'Ah baby, why can't they just do something? We have Jack, it won't come to that, you'll see, I have a good feeling about all of this.' She strokes his head, leaning in, kissing him softly. 'What date shall I state the commence?'

'It's his word against Jerry's, my sweater is.'

'Honestly you worry too much. Jack is the key to get you off.'

'Babe, you don't know the justice system like I do. Put the start date in from today, pay him weekly, you can have my assets and accounts. Pay him for looking after my offices, houses, collect rent from my house in London.'

'You've let it out already?'

'We've got this place.'

'Adam, I don't feel safe here. I'm driving to my parents' after you've gone back there. Which I am dead set against.'

'You're going to have to get used to it babe. Shall I buy you a place somewhere else?'

'No, this is a nightmare, here is fine. They're after Jack, not you and me.'

'Look after that bullet point, but he needs to drive you.'

'Drive me?'

'Yes.'

'No way am I having him as my driver.'

'Why not?'

'He's too young, and he still needs his social life even if you're getting him to do all of this.' She taps the Mac with her finger, laughing at all of Jack's new jobs.

'What you are giggling at?'

'All this is crazy work you're getting him to do, what

if you're acquitted? What are you going to do?'

'My job.'

'Who does all of this now for you?'

'Ah, about that.'

'Who?'

'Don't laugh.'

'Tell me?'

'Rebecca.'

'No! Ooh, ouch.'

'I had to get her out of that building, stop her working for him.'

'I get it but, what are we going to do, you're going to fire your sister?'

'Not exactly.'

'Then what?'

'Take out those three bullet points on this contract, it's too much for him. They can share. See, I think of everything.'

'Hmm, and you're paying him all of this amount to do just these?'

'Ah, said I would, let me go ask him. Can you take these out? Email or text him downstairs and I'll ask for a reconsideration of the pay.'

'Wait, what amount should I put on here?'

'Leave it blank. Say we're up here doing his contract and I'll be down in half an hour. Let me get that.' He slides the Mac off the bed and places it on the carpet. Then he pulls her into his arms, kissing her forehead, whispering, 'shall we?'

'Hmm, sounds good to me.'

'Wait – no, the baby.'

'Adam it's fine, we can have sex right up till I go into labour.'

'Really?'

'Yes, I've been researching it. It says the more we do it nearer the due date the better it is for bringing on the baby, boy or girl.'

'Both!'

'No, not twins!'

'Why?'

'Ha! I don't mind, I'm so excited.'

Adam's phone rings. 'Hello, yeah that's fine, thanks, bye.'

'Who was that?'

'The windows and doors are here.'

The phone rings again.

'Ah what now? One sec darling, I'll make this quick.' He kisses her on her head and answers the phone. 'Get here now!' It's Detective Thomas screaming down the receiver. Adam runs downstairs. Sophia sighs, picks up her Mac, eats a banana, drinks a glass of water, presses send.

Text from Jack: *There isn't a figure. Come down, why isn't there the figure he promised me? Jack xx.*

Sophia gets off the bed and goes through the door left ajar by Adam, who has run off like a madman.

She glimpses Maria packing her suitcase and cursing to herself in Spanish. Casually walking downstairs, she hears Detective Sergeant Thomas: 'We've got them in custody, Jerry and Williams.'

And Adam's response: 'Well how? When? Where?'

'Ah Sophia, you look better. We arrested them in his office, sound devices caught them. We heard that Williams was going to arrest Jack when he comes back on duty on Sunday. He was going to slip something in his drink, kill him off. We heard Jerry transferring half a million into his account, it's all on his laptop.'

Adam picks Sophia up, swirling her around the marble centre reception hall.

'Yes, yes, yes! Everyone in there now!' screams Adam.

Builders walk through with their tools, perplexed looks on their faces. Maria runs down, while Dave, Mick, Jack and Terry are meeting in the hall.

'All in there, now!' shouts Adam again. They walk into the large main lounge, closing the door behind everyone.

'It's over, they arrested Jerry and Williams, we're free.' Adam laughs out loud.

'Is my contract still happening?' Everyone's laughing. Maria hugs Sophia, the guys are shaking each other's hands, Mick hugging Terry.

'Oi get off me! Only joking, come here.' Thomas leaves the room and laughs, closing the door behind him.

Sophia opens the gilded gates and pulls into her

parent's driveway. She picks up her black Gucci bag from the passenger's seat, walks into the oval archway doors, puts her bag on the floor and places the fresh flowers in the vase. Austin runs out of the kitchen door and hugs her tightly.

'Wow, you look amazing sis! How are you? Mum and dad told me everything, we've just seen the news, come on, look it is all over the TV.'

'Austin you look terrible, look how skinny you are, are you...?'

Liz interjects, 'Oh darling, give me a hug, let me look at you, oh my, you're glowing.'

'Mother.'

'Are you...?'

'Shh, not now, where is dad?'

'Out, love. Water?'

'Yes please. Austin, I want to hear everything, are you off that ice stuff?'

CHAPTER 56

✦✦✦✦

Adam pulls over outside the two penthouse apartments Kenny had bought for Maria ten years before, knowing she was loyal, dedicated and in love with him but he couldn't reciprocate. Maria gave one to her sister Pita, but Pita decided to go to Australia with her husband, unwilling to have anything to do with her sister while she was working for the O'Connors.

'Thank you, Adam, tell James I work tomorrow. Bye for now, it's been so emotional.'

'See you around Maria, get some rest.'

As Maria kicks off her Jimmy Choos, she hears a noise from the other apartment. She runs across the landing and bangs on the door.

'*Pita, eres tu*?'

'*Si*.' Pita opens the door and hugs her sister, asking

question after question, holding her shoulders away from her to get a closer look, pulling her in, kissing her twenty times, screaming all sorts in Spanish. Pita, brown wavy long hair, olive skin blue big eyes, a mole on the side of her full lips, gestures to Maria to sit next to the small glass table with matching glass chairs. She pours orange juice into two glasses.

'*Todo ahora?* Want to know everything?

Hitmen are sitting in a variety of cars surrounding the whole MGM area, down the side roads and main roads, all eyes watching for Andrew and his men, knowing a shipment is being sent in an hour to Ireland. James has his brothers armed, watching at the port in Malaga, ready to shoot.

The Colombians are sitting in their apartments wanting to get a shot at Andrew, using infra-red binoculars, studying the cars. They see casually dressed men with semi-automatics at their sides. The feds – got to be. All are wondering who the people in cars are, the men who are also watching the shipping container.

Not knowing what's going on, Adam decides to get a coffee at his local harbour restaurant in Marbella. He is sitting out on the deck, sipping an espresso, taking in the view, watching the sunset. He books a hotel on the app, not wanting to go to an empty home.

Text to Sophia: *Are you home yet? A x*

Text to Adam: *Just arrived, Austin is back and mother fussing as per, are you okay? Xx*

Adam: *Having a coffee, booking a hotel x*

Sophia: *Why a hotel? Xx*

Adam: *Just because x*

Sophia: *I worry about you over there, be careful, I love you xx*

Adam: *I'm fine, don't worry, you'll see, I am only here for 24 hours, I love you too and our bump, xx*

Sophia: *It's probably the size of a pea! Xx*

Adam: *Ha! Cannot believe those tests can be so precise, goosebumps still X*

He decides to drive to Malaga, nearer the airport, and dials his client to have the meeting tonight, so he can get back first thing in the morning. Then he dials James at the gym, presses the button on the steering wheel and hangs up, knowing it's unsafe to discuss business. He wipes his brow and heads towards MGM before he can get his head down and have a good night's sleep.

He pulls into the familiar street; there are few cars. He switches off the engine, rolls his neck around, sighing, takes out his briefcase and opens the car door, walking up the steps. Lorraine is on reception, smiling and speaking fast with an Irish accent. 'Hey, what are you up to?'

'Hi, good to see you again, is he in?'

'That Kenny left a right mess in his office, taken me all day cleaning. There were so many messes, how did he live in there like that? You know Adam, James is going a tad crazy, won't tell me what on earth is going on. Oh Jesus please spare us.'

'Lorraine, it's all going to be fine.'

'How can you say that, three of my brothers in law have been…'

James opens the door and signals Adam to go inside. 'She can talk for hours, that one. What are you up to? Come inside, we have a lot going on, come here you.' He slaps Adam's back and they walk into the clearly lit office.

'Here, can I get you a drink?'

'Water please.'

'Have something stronger, you're with us, here.'

He slides an empty crystal glass over the table, pours an inch of scotch into his and passes the decanter across the table, holding it in the air. Adam reaches across and takes it out of his hand, pours a shot in his glass.

'Cheers, cheers.' They raise their glasses. 'James, what am I doing here, what do you need?

'Ah, good to see you me old china. Here, you know we've got a hit on. Andrew's out tonight, the fuckwit, you have to stay for a week, can you do that?'

'If it's necessary, sure.'

'Oh, it's going to be.'

'You know he won't leave his villa.'

'Ah fuck, you're right. I have all me men at the port watching the container, they're going to have to raid it.'

'Raid the container?'

'No, the villa. Let's drive to the port. We can't call them, the feds probably have my phone bugged.'

'I think that that's an understatement.'

'Cheeky fucker.'

'So, I'm staying to get you off for assassinating the Kelly family?'

'That's the deal, how much?'

'Two million.'

'Here, I'll transfer now. It's in.'

Adam's phone beeps: 'BANK' flashes. He uses his thumb print to open the bank app, smiles back at James.

'I haven't done anything yet.'

'Ah, but you will. Let's go, Adam, you drive.'

'I have a hotel near the port, meet you there.'

'Fine, we got security everywhere, not like Ken, didn't use his nut, poor sod. Now we're all here to take out the Kelly's once and for all. Here, put these on your shirt.'

Adam sits in the car and puts the gold cufflinks on, then chucks his silver ones in the leather dashboard ashtray. He pulls away, looking from side to side, checking the rear mirror. Cars overtaking, showing their armour. He looks behind to see the others in tow, knowing they're being secured along the way. He presses his lips together and shakes his head. *What have I set myself up for?*

He puts the earpiece in his ear, hearing voices, but not making sense out of the muffled sounds:

'I am leaving him after the port and going to the hotel. You hear me?'

'Ten four James, what's up?'

'Pull up behind the small café, Paseo del Muelle Uno.'

'I know it, why there?'

'Word is he's on his way there.'

'Andrew Kelly?'

'Yes, who else do you think I'm on about?'

'No, you're paying me to get you off in court, not to be a part of it.'

'Ah, you'll be all right.'

'James, how can I get you off if I am at the scene?'

'We're not doing him in the café, we're waiting till he gets on his ship. He won't go in the café, he'll drive straight to his cargo, won't he?'

'Ah fine, I'll have a coffee with you in there.'

'I'm not getting my hands dirty. He will be taken out by...'

'I get it.'

Adam scratches his chin and pulls into the car park, and several cars surround them. James gets out, but nobody else moves out of the cars. James and Adam walk inside. Adam takes the earpiece out, not wanting to hear any of it.

'Word is he is three miles away.'

'We're staying in here.'

'So we are, here you lot get in there now.'

The security all gathers inside the café, leave the cars so Andrew won't suspect anything. The two waitresses look perplexed, seeing everyone with semi-automatic rifles.

They whisper to each other and go into the back room, shutting the door.

There are cars on either side of Andrew, pulling into the side road of the café. The Colombians on their balconies watch Andrew get out, and the hitmen in the café start shooting. Glass shatters, the Colombians start shooting at Andrew, bullets are coming straight through the café.

Within seconds, Andrew and his bodyguards are dead on the concrete. Then it's the hitmen's turn to start falling one by one as the Colombians fire from further away, measured shots, non-stop.

Adam dropped to the floor for cover as soon as the firing began, but when it stops at last, he does not get up, does not stir, and the light from the café windows catches the glint of dark blood pooling under his chest.

In the distance, the sirens begin, first one, then two, then many, until the walls echo to the sound of their orchestra.